For Danielle Butchart
and
Ellie Butchart

x x x

D0353571

First published in the UK in 2017 by Nosy Crow Ltd
The Crow's Nest, 14 Baden Place, Crosby Row,
London, SE1 1YW, UK

Nosy Crow and associated logos are trademarks and/or registered
trademarks of Nosy Crow Ltd

Text copyright © Pamela Butchart, 2017
Cover and illustrations copyright © Thomas Flintham, 2017

The right of Pamela Butchart and Thomas Flintham to be identified
as the author and illustrator respectively of this work has been asserted
by them in accordance with the Copyright, Designs
and Patents Act 1988.

7 9 10 8 6

A CIP catalogue record for this book will be available from the British Library.

Printed and bound in the UK by Clays Ltd, St. Ives Plc

Papers used by Nosy Crow are made from wood grown in
sustainable forests.

ISBN: 978 0 85763 906 6

www.nosycrow.com

Contents

Lucky to be Alive!

When we found out that we were going on a school camping trip for FOUR WHOLE NIGHTS we were MEGA excited.

But that's because we didn't know about the WEIRD HOWLING at night and THE GLOWING EYES and our PE teacher's

1

HAIRY LEGS!
And we **DEFINITELY** didn't know that we were going to get

LOST IN THE WILDERNESS

and have to become

SURVIVAL EXPERTS.

Maisie said that she knew something **BAD** was going to happen on the camping trip and that she had felt it in her **BONES** and that's why she brought the **BEAR SPRAY.**

Zach said that we probably should have paid a bit more attention to things instead of being OBSESSED with SECURING the back seat of the bus.

And Jodi says that we are all lucky to be alive and she is right because I don't think a lot of people who wake up to find a werewolf in their tent live to tell the tale.

But we did.

Into
the
WILDERNESS

When we went to school on Monday, Miss Jones made us all sit down because she said she had some IMPORTANT NEWS.

My friend Maisie gripped my hand under the table and I knew she thought it was going to be BAD NEWS because Maisie

ALWAYS thinks bad things are going to happen because she is a WORRIER. But I suppose I can't really blame her because

WEIRD STUFF

does seem to happen a lot at our school. Like the times with the French spy and the vampire rats and all the demon dinner ladies!

But then Miss Jones said, "Do you remember you asked if we could all go on a school trip?"

Everyone STARED at each other and then

at Miss Jones and said, "Yeeees?"

Then Miss Jones said, "Perhaps even stay overnight somewhere?"

And everyone gasped and said, **"YEEEEEEES??!"**

Miss Jones said, "Well, guess what? We're going on a CAMPING TRIP for FOUR WHOLE NIGHTS!"

EVERYONE started screaming and running around, and Nola Burke even started

crying with happiness, because we had **NEVER** been on an **OVERNIGHT** school trip before and it was going to be

AWESOME!

Jodi (that's my friend) stared at me with her mouth wide open and said, "I can't believe this is actually happening!"

NO ONE could concentrate on doing their maths that morning because **EVERYONE** was talking about who was going to sit at the back of the bus.

Jodi said that she would get her mum to drop us off at school at 5am so that we could be at the front of the bus queue and get the back seat. But that's when Maisie gripped my arm really tightly and said that we had more

IMPORTANT

things to worry about because we were going **CAMPING** which meant we were going to

have to sleep in a TENT and be in the

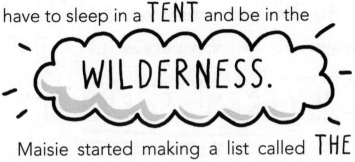

WILDERNESS.

Maisie started making a list called THE DANGER LIST and she wrote LOADS of stuff on it like:

POISONOUS SPIDERS

BEARS

NO TOILETS

But Jodi said that she had watched all of Season One **AND** Season Two of

"EXTREME SURVIVAL"

which was all about what to do in the

so that you didn't die. And that made Maisie feel better so she stopped doing the list.

Then I put up my hand and asked Miss Jones what teachers would be coming on the trip with us.

Miss Jones said, "Well, I'll be there, and so will your new PE teacher. Her name is Miss Moon. Camping was her idea, actually."

Zach gasped and covered his mouth with his hands and Maisie almost jumped out of her skin because of how loud the gasp was.

Then Zach said, "Miss Moon is the SCARIEST PE teacher EVER!"

He said that he heard Miss Moon made one of the Year 6s run BAREFOOT in the playground in the RAIN when they forgot their trainers and that she didn't accept NOTES and that she made you do PE anyway, even if both of your arms were broken.

And that's when Maisie said she

DEFINITELY

wasn't going.

The Bus Sofa

On the day of the school trip Miss Jones said that we were to meet at school at 8am, but Jodi made us be there at 7.15am SHARP. That way we would DEFINITELY get the big long seat at the very back also known as the Bus Sofa.

Jodi's mum stayed with us until Miss Jones got there and then Jodi hugged her mum for a really long time until her mum left because she had to get to work.

When Zach got there, Jodi gave him a LOOK and tapped her watch with her finger because it was no longer 7.15am SHARP, it was now 7.42am.

Miss Jones told us to all go to the toilet before the bus got there. So we told Zach that he had to stand in the Bus Stop Spot until we got back and then we ran as fast as we could to the toilet. And Jodi wouldn't even let me wash my hands after because she shouted, "It's HERE! I can HEAR IT!" and then she squirted ANTI-BACTERIAL GEL on my hands and pulled me out the door.

When we got back outside, LOADS of people were there with all their tent stuff and sleeping bags and Gary Petrie had brought his Star Wars duvet and he was running around waving it at everyone.

That's when Jodi said, "I'm going to KILL HIM!"

I thought she meant Gary Petrie but then I noticed that Zach wasn't standing at the Bus Stop Spot any more.

Jodi RAN down the steps and waved at the driver to open the bus doors. But the driver just kept on reading his newspaper.

The doors made a weird noise when he eventually opened them and a REALLY TALL woman with a LONG NOSE stepped out and said, "Hello there. I'm Miss Moon. And I'm very happy to meet you."

I was shocked because of the TALLNESS.

And Jodi must have been too because we both just stood there **STARING** at Miss Moon and not saying anything until we heard Zach yell, "Help!" and we turned and saw him trying to get Maisie and all her camping stuff out of her mum's car.

Maisie's backpack was **MUCH** bigger than she was and it had at least **FOUR** sleeping bags and loads of pillows strapped to it.

17

In the end, we had to carry Maisie and her backpack from the car to the bus. But when we tried to stand her up straight she kept toppling backwards so we just had to lay her down on the pavement.

Jodi said that maybe we should take some of the sleeping bags off but then Miss Moon appeared and whipped Maisie up, took her backpack off and threw it in the luggage bit of the bus with

ONE HAND,

saying, "There you go!"

We all stared up at Miss Moon and Maisie gulped a bit.

Miss Moon looked even TALLER than before.

We all just stood there and watched Miss Moon as she started grabbing EVERYONE'S bags and throwing them into the luggage bit.

That's when Zach said, "She's strong!" And we nodded because she was probably the strongest (and tallest!) lady we had ever seen!

When it was time for us to go, Maisie's mum wouldn't stop hugging Maisie and calling her

MY LITTLE ANGEL WINGS

so we had to peel her arms off and promise her that we would take VERY GOOD CARE of Maisie and make sure that she used all her sleeping bags and wore all of her socks.

When we eventually got on the bus Jodi RAN to the back as fast as she could and spread her coat and her hoodie over all the back seats and then shouted down to us that she had "SECURED THE AREA".

As soon as Gary Petrie EVENTUALLY let Miss Jones put his Star Wars duvet in the luggage bit and got on the bus, we were off!

Me and Zach opened the little curtains at the back of bus and waved goodbye to all the mums and dads. That's when I noticed that both my mum AND Zach's mum were holding on to Maisie's mum. But then Maisie's mum broke free and started running after the bus so I just quickly shut the bus curtains before Maisie could see.

We all listened as Miss Moon started telling us the Bus Rules. But she went ON and ON about LITTER for ages so we just started taking all of our Bus Snacks out of our bags and showing each other what we had.

But Miss Moon must have noticed because her voice went a bit angry and she said, "Can you HEAR me at the back?" So we all shouted,

"YES!"

Once Miss Moon was finished Maisie let out a BIG BREATH and that's when I realised that she had been holding her breath the whole time Miss Moon was talking because she was obviously a bit scared of Miss Moon because of her ANGRY VOICE and also because she was so tall that her head was almost touching the roof of the bus. When everyone got out their Bus Snacks, Zach said that he thought we should share and I knew that he said it because he wanted to share MAISIE'S Bus Snacks because she had LOADS and they all looked really good.

Once we'd finished our Bus Snacks, Zach said that he felt a bit sick and me and Jodi gave him a LOOK because we had made a PROMISE that we wouldn't mention feeling sick or ANYTHING because Maisie gets really bad TRAVEL SICKNESS and we didn't want her to be sick all over us.

But then Maisie rolled up her sleeves and showed us her ANTI-SICKNESS BRACELETS. Maisie said that they did something to your wrists and your BRAIN that stopped you from being sick and you were supposed to wear just ONE but her mum had bought her TWELVE and that she was wearing them all so that she

DEFINITELY couldn't be sick.

Zach said that he really wanted to find out what Miss Moon was like and we all agreed. So we sent Zach down to the front of the bus to ask Miss Moon a FAKE QUESTION (which is a question that you don't really need to know the answer to but you just pretend that you do so you can go wherever the teacher is and see stuff).

I told Zach that he should ask Miss Jones about what we do with our LITTER. But Zach said that he didn't want to ask that because he would get told off for not listening to Miss Moon.

So I waited for Jodi to suggest a FAKE QUESTION because she always likes to tell us what to do, but she didn't say ANYTHING, and that's when I realised that she had been really quiet since the bus left which was a bit weird because Jodi is never quiet.

But before I could ask Jodi about that, Maisie said, "Ask her about Toilet Breaks." Zach said that was a

fake question. But then Maisie shook her head and her face went a bit green and that's when we realised that it WASN'T a fake question and that Maisie really DID need to know the answer to the question because she was about to be sick!

The Biggest Tent in the WORLD!

I was TOTALLY EXCITED when I saw our campsite because it was even BETTER than I'd imagined and it had a HUGE forest all around it and a SHOP and Miss Jones said we could pitch our tents ANYWHERE we liked because we had the whole tent bit to ourselves!

Me, Zach, Jodi and Maisie all ran to the bit by some trees because the trees were bendy and they were like a big Tree Umbrella. Jodi said that it was the perfect spot because it gave us protection from

THE ELEMENTS

and I knew that meant that the Tree Umbrella would protect us from the RAIN and WIND because Jodi had been going on about THE ELEMENTS ever since she found out we were going camping.

As soon as we started unpacking the tents, Jodi started saying LOADS of stuff that she'd learned from watching

"EXTREME SURVIVAL",

like "THE GREAT OUTDOORS" and "ALWAYS RESPECT NATURE" and "PROTEIN BAR".

It took us AGES to work out how to unpack our tent because Jodi's mum had got us

THE BIGGEST TENT

EVER.

It had THREE bedrooms and it even had a LIVING ROOM BIT.

Zach had brought his own tent and when he laid it out next to ours it looked TINY.

It actually looked more like a sleeping bag than a tent! But then Jodi said that it had been very PROFESSIONAL of Zach to bring a

SURVIVAL

tent and that made Zach happy.

Miss Moon said that we shouldn't try to put our tents up until she came around with her SAFETY HAMMER. But Jodi didn't want to wait, and she'd already taken her OWN hammer out of her bag and was making us hold down the pegs while she hammered them in.

I had to close my eyes when Jodi was hammering in the peg that I was holding because I was terrified that she was going to WHACK me!

That's when Miss Moon shouted,

"HALT, CAMPER!"

and came running over and SNATCHED the hammer out of Jodi's hand and said that it was DANGEROUS and AGAINST THE RULES and that pupils were definitely NOT allowed to bring hammers with them.

Once we EVENTUALLY got the tent up we pulled all our stuff inside and started setting out our sleeping bags.

That's when Jodi asked Maisie if she had a plaster because she'd got a scratch on her hand from Miss Moon's SUPER LONG NAILS when Miss Moon had SNATCHED her hammer away.

Maisie said that she had LOADS of plasters and tipped out her whole backpack to find them.

I couldn't BELIEVE how much stuff came out of Maisie's backpack!

She had brought:

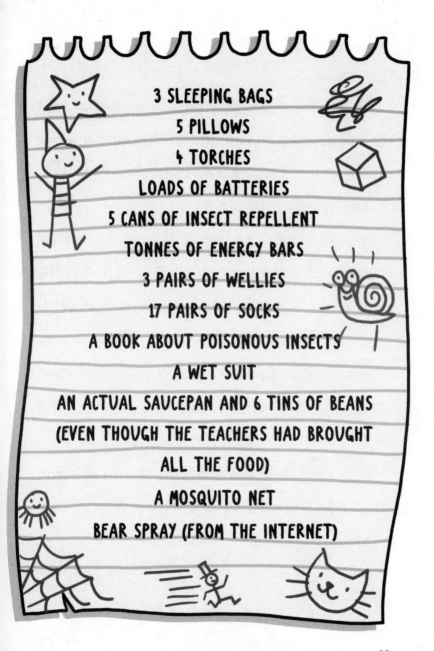

3 SLEEPING BAGS

5 PILLOWS

4 TORCHES

LOADS OF BATTERIES

5 CANS OF INSECT REPELLENT

TONNES OF ENERGY BARS

3 PAIRS OF WELLIES

17 PAIRS OF SOCKS

A BOOK ABOUT POISONOUS INSECTS

A WET SUIT

AN ACTUAL SAUCEPAN AND 6 TINS OF BEANS

(EVEN THOUGH THE TEACHERS HAD BROUGHT

ALL THE FOOD)

A MOSQUITO NET

BEAR SPRAY (FROM THE INTERNET)

That's when Jodi said that we were going to have to use one of the bedrooms to store Maisie's stuff because we could hardly MOVE in the living room bit.

So we moved all the stuff and I said that I would share a Tent Bedroom with Maisie and that Jodi could have a Tent Bedroom to herself, and I could see that Maisie was really happy about that and I knew that it was because she was scared about sleeping on her own.

Jodi said that she was a hundred per cent sure that you didn't get bears in Scotland but Maisie said that it was better to be SAFE than SORRY and she put the can of BEAR SPRAY under her pillow.

Then all of a sudden we heard THUNDER and the rain started to POUR down on to our tent and loads of people started screaming.

We unzipped the front door so we could poke our heads out and watched as everyone ran around grabbing their stuff and diving into their tents.

Except for Miss Moon.

She just stood under a tiny umbrella in the middle of the campsite STARING at the barbecue and she looked

REALLY WEIRD.

That's when Jodi said, "What is she DOING?"

But I had NO IDEA because the rain got so heavy that we couldn't really see her properly.

Maisie started FREAKING OUT because she said that she'd never seen rain as heavy as THIS rain before and that it was probably a STORM or even a HURRICANE.

Zach said that he hoped it WAS a hurricane because then maybe they would name it after one of us and then he started saying

HURRICANE ZACH

in a loud booming voice over and over until he realised that Maisie had fainted.

Hurricane Zach

Even though we were TRAPPED in our tent by Hurricane Zach I was still having a really good time because I thought it was actually really EXCITING being in a tent in the middle of a storm and I kept getting the giggles.

We zipped Maisie up in one of her sleeping bags and put the hood bit up so she was nice and cosy because that's really all you can do when Maisie faints because of FEAR.

Jodi said we should make a SURVIVAL PLAN because of the STORM but Zach said we should tell GHOST STORIES instead because it was a bit dark because of the rain and also because we had loads of snacks and all of Maisie's torches so we could make our faces look all scary.

But Jodi said that she wasn't really in the mood for ghost stories which was

MEGA WEIRD

because Jodi is usually ALWAYS in the mood for ghost stories.

So that's when Zach said that he knew a really good TRUE story that wasn't a ghost story and that it was a PERFECT time to tell it because Maisie was still having a little Fainting Nap so she wouldn't hear and get scared and faint again.

So I got into my sleeping bag, even though it was still the afternoon, and opened a

SHERBERT DIP.

Zach shone a torch under his chin and tried to make himself look all scary. But me and Jodi BURST out laughing because he was shining it up his nose and lighting up all his nose hairs.

So Zach moved the torch a bit and then he said, "Once upon a time, there was a very TALL lady called ... um ... Miss TROON and she had a LONG nose and scratchy CLAWS."

I looked at Jodi and she rolled her eyes at me because we both knew Zach was just making this TRUE STORY up as he went along and that Miss TROON was obviously Miss MOON.

Then Zach said, "Miss Troon was a RAIN SORCERER who could summon the rain whenever she wanted. But one day, she summoned the rain a bit too much and HURRICANE ZACH arrived and—"

But Zach didn't get to finish his sentence because that's when the whole tent started

SHAKING.

At first we thought it was the STORM making the tent shake but then we looked at Maisie and saw that she was awake and it was her doing the shaking.

I thought Maisie was shaking because she had heard Zach's not-a-ghost-story but then she pointed at the tent door and that's when I SCREAMED because there was a FLOATING FACE!

I got such a fright that I panicked and threw my Sherbet Dip at the FLOATING FACE and THAT made the face look even SCARIER because the Sherbet Dip EXPLODED all over the floating face and

made it look like a

GHOST FACE.

And that's when Zach started screaming too, and Maisie fainted again. But then the Ghost Face started coughing and Jodi pushed it out of the tent and zipped the tent back up.

Jodi said that it had just been Gary Petrie and that we should probably use her mini-padlock to LOCK our tent so he didn't steal all of our snacks.

And then ANOTHER FACE APPEARED!

But it was only Miss Jones telling us to come for dinner.

Miss Moon was DETERMINED to do the barbecue and she made us all stand in the rain for AGES while she tried to light it before Miss Jones said, "That's it! We're going to the restaurant for dinner."

But when we got to the restaurant the waitress said that there were no burgers OR sausages OR steak left and that there was only the VEGETARIAN OPTION left.

None of us were bothered because the vegetarian option was PIZZA. But Miss

Moon made a **BIG FUSS** about there not being any **MEAT** left and she wouldn't have any pizza and she just sat there looking angry and saying that everyone should have let her try **ONE MORE TIME** to get the barbecue working because then we could have all had sausages and burgers.

Miss Jones didn't say anything. She just gave Miss Moon a **LOOK**. It was like the look Miss Jones gave me one time when she asked me to **CAREFULLY** hold her handbag when I wasn't doing swimming because of my **TOENAIL ISSUE** and I **ACCIDENTALLY** dropped it in the pool.

Maisie whispered, "Miss Moon is a bit of a moan, isn't she?"

And we all agreed because she DEFINITELY WAS and the whole

FREAKING OUT

because she couldn't have any MEAT thing was a bit ridiculous.

We said that Zach could come into our tent before bed so that we could all tell stories and eat snacks and also because we needed his help to get Maisie's MOSQUITO NET up.

It took ages to get Maisie inside all of her sleeping bags because one of them had all these complicated bits that Maisie's legs and arms had to go into and once she was all zipped up it sort of looked like a SPACE SUIT.

Maisie said that she was too sleepy and TOO TERRIFIED to tell ghost stories so we just put her EYE MASK on and made sure she had her WAX EARPLUGS in.

Me and Jodi and Zach sat in the living room bit with the torches. Jodi was being very quiet which was a bit weird because one time when I was at her house I actually had to put my HAND UP because she wouldn't stop talking and I wanted to say something.

Zach said that he was going to go back to his own tent because he was tired but he was going to check if Miss Moon was still trying to get the barbecue to work first because he was a bit hungry for barbecue. It was TOTALLY DARK outside so me and Jodi said that we would just stay in the tent and that when Zach got into his tent he should use his torch to SIGNAL to us by FLASHING THREE TIMES.

So we waited. But Zach didn't do ANY flashes.

So we waited more.

But then Jodi said that almost TEN MINUTES had passed and that something must have gone WRONG and that ZACH had probably wandered off

INTO THE WILDERNESS.

I said that we needed to go out and find Zach RIGHT AWAY because I didn't like the idea of him being lost in the scary woods by himself.

But then Jodi said that one of us had to stay with Maisie because if she woke up on her own she would

FREAK OUT.

I knew Jodi was right but I was too scared to go out on my own so I didn't say anything and Jodi didn't say anything either. So we just sat there and waited for Zach to do the FLASHES.

Howling
in the
Night

When I woke up I had **NO IDEA** where I was and everything was **PITCH BLACK**.

But then I heard Maisie snoring and remembered that I was in a tent and that we were camping.

Then I remembered that we weren't

supposed to be sleeping because we were waiting for Zach to do the FLASHES!

I was JUST about to wake Jodi up to tell her we had fallen asleep when I remembered what had woken me up.

HOWLING.

I'd heard HOWLING!

I froze. I was too scared to move so I just lay there and listened. But I couldn't hear anything except Maisie snoring.

I whispered to Jodi but she didn't answer. I felt around with my hands to see if she was lying next to me but there was no one there.

And THAT'S when I started to panic because Jodi must have gone out searching for Zach by HERSELF and now they were BOTH lost in the woods! I had to do something (even if there WAS a scary howling beast thing LURKING outside)!

So that's when I put my torch on and looked around. Jodi DEFINITELY wasn't there.

I was JUST about to wake up Maisie and tell her we had a BIG PROBLEM when I noticed a LUMP in the other bedroom bit.

I shone the torch on the lump and my heart almost fell out of my body because the lump WASN'T Jodi.

The lump was HUGE and DARK and FUZZY!

And that's when I realised where the howling had come from.

THERE'S A WILD BEAST IN OUR TENT!

I was **JUST** about to scream when Jodi's **SURVIVAL TRAINING** kicked in and I realised that if I did, I'd probably get eaten by the wild beast. So I didn't.

Jodi said once that when something bad happens, people can either **FIGHT** or

FLIGHT (means that they run away so fast that it looks like they're flying).

I counted to five really slowly in my head and made a FLIGHT PLAN.

I was going to grab Maisie and RUN. But then I realised that I wouldn't be able to get past Maisie's mosquito net and get her out of her SPACE SUIT SLEEPING BAG without making a lot of noise and waking up

THE BEAST.

So I made a FIGHT PLAN instead.

I was going to TRAP THE BEAST and THEN get Maisie out safely.

I crawled REALLY slowly and REALLY quietly across the tent towards Jodi's backpack.

I could feel my heart beating in my throat as I searched inside for the mini-padlock.

I kept my eyes on

at all times. Which made it hard to search the rucksack, but Jodi had said to MAINTAIN EYE CONTACT AT ALL TIMES when faced with a wild animal.

I almost cried out with happiness when I felt the cold metal of the mini suitcase padlock with my fingers.

But then Maisie did a louder snorty thing and

THE BEAST

moved a bit so that's when I LEAPT across the tent and zipped up the door to the BEAST'S bedroom bit and put the little padlock through the zips and snapped it shut.

Then I LEAPT into the other bedroom bit and started pulling Maisie out of the tent by her feet because that was going to be quicker than trying to get her out of the SPACE SUIT SLEEPING BAG.

But then Maisie started SCREAMING because she had NO IDEA what was going on as she still had her eye mask and earplugs in.

And that's when

woke up and started trying to get out of the bedroom bit. So I got Maisie out of the tent and into the long grass before unzipping her and shouting for Miss Jones at the TOP OF MY VOICE!

⭐

The next morning, Miss Jones and Miss Moon looked really tired and annoyed.

And I knew that it was because we had woken up THE WHOLE CAMP in the middle of the night.

Miss Jones had **NOT** been pleased about the screaming coming from Maisie **OR** the fact that Zach was almost crying because he had been zipped up in the bedroom bit of the tent. She **ALSO** wasn't pleased that Jodi and Zach had switched tents without permission and neither was I because if Jodi had just **WOKEN ME UP AND TOLD ME** that Zach had come to our tent to tell us that his torch had run out of batteries so he couldn't do the flashing, and that he was too scared to sleep in the **SURVIVAL TENT** by himself and that Jodi had then switched tents with him because she was **NOT** scared then **I DEFINITELY WOULDN'T** have thought that Zach with his big hairy blanket thing was a

WILD BEAST

and I wouldn't have given myself and Maisie and Miss Jones such a fright.

Jodi thought the whole thing was hilarious. But I didn't because even though the hairy lump had just turned out to be Zach that still didn't explain the **HOWLING** I had heard that had woken me up in the first place.

Jodi said I had probably just DREAMT IT ALL and that really ANNOYED me because, like I said, I think I know the difference between hearing something in REAL LIFE and DREAMING IT.

But then Jodi said that she hadn't heard a thing and neither had Maisie but I knew that Maisie had been wearing earplugs made from real beeswax so she wouldn't have heard even if

THE BEAST

had howled RIGHT in her ear.

Then Jodi asked Zach and he said that he hadn't heard any howling in the night but that he had heard a SNUFFLING sound outside the tent but that he just thought it had been a dog.

I STARED at Zach because he had OBVIOUSLY forgotten that we were on a CAMPSITE and that we were the

ONLY PEOPLE THERE

and that we hadn't brought a dog with us.

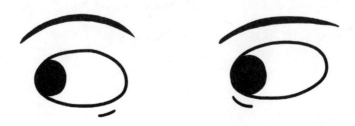

That's when Jodi said that maybe there were people in the CARAVAN bit who had a dog. And I knew that made sense but I still had a WEIRD feeling about the HOWLING. Plus, Jodi had been acting a bit weirdly since we got on the bus so I knew that she wasn't really paying attention to the EVIDENCE properly.

Then when we were all having our cereal together Maisie said, "Miss Jones. Are there WOLVES in those woods?"

Miss Moon STOOD UP really SLOWLY and got a WEIRD LOOK on her face and, "Are you asking about WOLVES?"

We all looked up at Miss Moon (which took a few seconds because of how tall Miss Moon is, especially when you are sitting down). Maisie's spoon started hitting the side of her cereal bowl and we all knew it was because she was shaking because she was scared of Miss Moon and how tall she was.

So then I put my hand on Maisie's hand to stop the shaking and I said, "Maisie was just asking if you get wolves here, because, um, I heard something last night."

Miss Jones said that there were

NO WOLVES

here and that it was probably just the WIND I had heard the night before.

Zach asked Miss Jones if she was SURE because he thought this would be the PERFECT PLACE for wolves because of how THICK the forest was and that wolves would probably love roaming and hiding here.

Then Miss Moon said, "Miss Jones is quite right that there are no wolves here. But there USED to be. The last wolf in Scotland was seen in these actual woods. And someone wants to release wolves back into the Scottish countryside. Isn't that a GREAT IDEA? I think wolves are WONDERFUL CREATURES!" And she smiled a REALLY WEIRD smile.

I was just about to say that it WASN'T a good idea at ALL and that it was TERRIFYING instead when I noticed that

Maisie was going a bit SWIRLY in the eyes so I changed the subject and asked what we were doing after breakfast.

That's when Miss Moon got really excited and she told us about the SCAVENGER HUNT.

Miss Moon said that she'd woken up at 5am and laid a scavenger hunt around the WHOLE campsite and that the team that completed the scavenger hunt first would win a PRIZE!

Miss Jones said that we had to get into teams of four and decide a LEADER and before we could even say ONE WORD Jodi shouted,

"ME! I'M THE LEADER!"

The Scavenger Hunt

Jodi DRAGGED us into the woods to look for the first items on the SCAVENGER-HUNT LIST because she LOVES games and competitions like that.

I wasn't sure if Maisie was going to be OK because she kept saying that this was the

VERY FIRST TIME she had ever been in

THE WILDERNESS

and also because she wouldn't open her eyes so she kept bumping into everything.

It was easy to find the first couple of things on the scavenger-hunt list because the first item was a LEAF and the second item was an ACORN.

But then Maisie said, "What are THOSE?!"

And I looked up and saw that Maisie was pointing to a tree covered in SCRATCHES.

Me and Zach went over to investigate and

that's when we saw how DEEP the scratches were.

I looked at Zach and he looked at me and I just KNEW that he was thinking the same thing as me. And that the thing he was thinking was

WILD BEAST!

But then Jodi shouted that we had to PAY ATTENTION to the scavenger hunt because Jodi is VERY COMPETITIVE and one time when she didn't win the class Christmas Quiz her mum had to come and collect her because she got so mad she broke every single rubber in the Rubber Tray and Maisie said that she was lucky she didn't get EXPELLED.

So anyway, Jodi told us all to stop staring at the trees and help her to find a blueberry

☆ ASAP! ☆

But when we were looking in the BUSH BIT for a blueberry Maisie SCREAMED and pointed to something and I thought it was going to be more TREE SCRATCHES. But it wasn't. It was MUCH WORSE. Because it was a GIANT POO!

We all STARED at the giant poo because it was probably the biggest poo in the world. And even though it was COMPLETELY DISGUSTING we all couldn't stop looking at it and it was probably because we were in SHOCK.

Zach said that something REALLY BIG must have made it. And then he looked at me and gulped and I knew that it was because he was remembering the

TREE SCRATCHES
and the HOWLING.

But then Jodi picked up a broken branch covered with leaves and threw it over the giant poo so we couldn't see it any more and told us to FOCUS and also that it was probably just a really big dog that had done it or maybe even a horse.

So we all went to a different bit of the woods to look for a blueberry because no one wanted to look for blueberries in the Poo Bit.

After the blueberry, the Scavenger Hunt got harder because you had to solve a RIDDLE and the riddle said:

You'll find me standing tall,

Ready to take your call.

I had no idea what the riddle meant. But Maisie is very good at riddles and she said that it was definitely a PHONE BOX.

Jodi almost

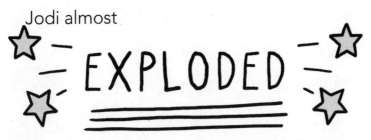
EXPLODED

with excitement when Maisie said that and then she shouted, **"THERE'S A PHONE BOX ON CAMP!!"** and then she GRABBED the map from my hand and pointed down towards the river.

I was surprised that Jodi was so excited about the PHONE BOX because she definitely hadn't been screaming about the LEAF or the ACORN!

Then Jodi said, "You know what, people? We might actually **WIN THIS THING!**" and then she grabbed our hands and we all ran towards the phone box.

The River Garry

When we got to the phone box Jodi went inside for AGES and it looked like she was trying to actually USE the phone so I banged on the glass to see if she'd found any clues but she shook her head to say she hadn't but she stayed in there anyway.

Then we heard someone SHOUTING and we saw Gary Petrie sitting on a sign at the entrance to the forest and shouting something at the rest of his group.

Jodi started walking towards Gary Petrie so I said, "Where are you GOING?" And Jodi said that she thought someone had TAKEN the PHONE-BOX CLUE so no one else could win. And that is EXACTLY what Gary Petrie is LIKE so we all marched over to where Gary's group was. When we got there we saw that the sign that Gary was sitting on said, "This Way to the River Garry" and he was doing loads of POSES on the sign and getting someone in his group to take pictures of him showing off.

Then he spotted us and said, "Thou cannot pass into MY forest."

So I said, "It's not YOUR forest!"

But Gary Petrie just pointed to the sign and said,

"Read it and WEEP!"

I was JUST about to tell Gary Petrie that he was more annoying than EVERYTHING when Jodi said, "ACTUALLY it's the RIVER that's called Garry. Not the forest."

Gary looked at the sign for a bit and then he said, "Well, thou cannot go into my RIVER, then."

And Jodi said, "That's fine by us because YOUR horrible river will obviously be pure freezing!"

But Gary said that it WASN'T and that it was probably as warm as a JACUZZI and that Miss Moon would probably let him go for a SWIM in his own river later.

That's when Jodi BURST out laughing and said that Gary obviously had NO IDEA about BODIES OF WATER.

Then Jodi went on for AGES about the

AVERAGE TEMPERATURES of rivers in Scotland and RAPIDS and DANGER and Gary Petrie looked SO CONFUSED that he didn't say anything back.

So that's when we asked about the Phone-Box Clue and Gary Petrie smiled a bit and said that he had NO IDEA what we were talking about which meant that he DEFINITELY DID know!

So Jodi stepped forward and gave him one of her LOOKS and Gary gulped because he's a bit scared of Jodi.

And then he said, "Um. The clue just said to look here, at this sign."

So Jodi stepped even closer to Gary Petrie and said, "OK. So show us what you found."

Gary Petrie got a weird look on his face and said, "Um ... well..." and we all realised that they hadn't actually FOUND the next item yet! And all of a sudden, Jodi dropped to the ground and crawled THROUGH Gary Petrie's legs and GRABBED something from under the sign and I saw that it was a RED GLOVE.

Maisie yelled, "The FINAL SCAVENGER ITEM!"

And Jodi ran.

Gary Petrie's group ran after Jodi because THEY wanted the RED GLOVE so THEY could win the scavenger hunt. But we knew that there was NO WAY they were going to catch Jodi because last year she actually won EVERY SINGLE PRIZE at Sports Day.

When we got back to camp, Miss Moon said we'd won the scavenger hunt and Gary Petrie was SO ANNOYED that he said he was going to his tent and that no one should disturb him

EVER.

So we said that we wouldn't let him know when lunch was ready and that's when he said that he'd changed his mind and that it was fine to disturb him if it was about food or more games or anything good.

Then Miss Moon said that it was time to

play **HOT CHOCOLATE RIVER** and Gary shouted,

"THE RIVER GARRY!"

Miss Moon said that two long ropes marked either side of the **HOT CHOCOLATE RIVER** and that we had to get from one side to the other using only **MARSHMALLOWS**.

Miss Jones handed everyone a **PAPER PLATE** and said we had to pretend they were marshmallows. She told us to use the paper plates to pass safely from one side of the hot chocolate river to the other. And she said that we had to keep a FOOT on the paper plates AT ALL TIMES or they would float away.

I just KNEW that we were going to lose the game because we were in a group with Gary Petrie and one of his annoying friends who'd just secretly stuffed about twenty cheese puffs into his mouth.

As soon as Miss Jones shouted, **"GO!"** all of the groups started using their paper plates to cross. That's when Cheese Puff Geoff shouted, **"COME ON!"** **RIGHT** in my ear and I screamed because he spat cheese dust **ALL OVER ME** and Maisie toppled off her paper plate and landed in the river. And even though it was only a **PRETEND** river Maisie screamed **SO LOUD** that it echoed through the forest and **EVERYONE** had to cover their ears.

Then Gary Petrie said, **"I'll SAVE HER! I HAVE THE POWER OF RIVER GARRY RUNNING THROUGH ME!"**

So Gary pretended to swim through the grass and he scooped Maisie up and helped her back on to a paper plate.

That's when Miss Moon came rushing over and said, "EXCELLENT team work! Well done everyone! Especially GARY!"

Gary Petrie started taking loads of bows and then he licked his finger and pointed it at the sky and shouted,

"THE POWER OF RIVER GARRY!"

And then he looked at Maisie and winked
and Maisie started giggling.

Miss Moon said we could have some
FREE TIME and then she got a REALLY
EXCITED LOOK on her face and told

us that there would DEFINITELY be a barbecue later and we all knew that she was excited because she was a bit OBSESSED with MEAT!

But then all of a sudden Zach RAN over to us and said we had to get to the tent ASAP!

And then he covered Maisie's ears with his hands and said, "Hurry! It's a

LEVEL ELEVEN EMERGENCY!"

A LEVEL ELEVEN EMERGENCY!

Zach uncovered Maisie's ears because she'd obviously heard him anyway because her eyes had gone all SWIRLY and then she'd sort of slumped against Zach and slid to the ground. And we all knew that Maisie had fainted because a Level Eleven Emergency is our code for an emergency that is even MORE serious than the usual most serious Level Ten Emergency!

Miss Moon came RACING over when she saw that Maisie had fainted, shouting,

"CAMPER DOWN! CAMPER DOWN!"

And Zach went REALLY WEIRD in the face. But we didn't know why.

Maisie opened her eyes and said that she was OK and that she just needed some fresh air so we all used our hands to fan air on to Maisie's face and hoped that Miss Moon would just go away so Zach could finish telling us what on EARTH was going on.

But Miss Moon was already on the ground next to Maisie checking her VITAL SIGNS and shining a torch into her eyes. And then she started asking Maisie how many fingers she was holding up and who the Prime Minister was. I didn't really think it was a good time to be giving Maisie a QUIZ since she'd just fainted but Maisie managed to get all the answers right and that made Miss Moon happy.

Then Miss Moon took her jacket off and put it over Maisie and told her to stay COMPLETELY STILL until she could LOCATE FRESH WATER. And then she ran off.

So we all asked Maisie if she was OK and Maisie nodded that she was, even though she was still lying on the ground in the RECOVERY POSITION with Miss Moon's jacket over her and bits of mud and twigs in her hair.

But then Maisie took a deep breath and said, "I'm fine. Really."And I smiled at her because she was being really brave and also because I wanted her to look at me and not at the beetle that was right beside her head.

Then Zach said, "COME ON! We have to get OUT OF HERE!"

So we picked up Maisie and we RAN.

When we got to the tent Zach looked a bit **WILD**. His hair was even messier than usual and he was muttering to himself as he rushed around packing a backpack until Jodi grabbed him by his shoulders and said, **"WHAT?!"**

But Zach said that he couldn't tell us here and that the **"WALLS HAVE EARS!"** and even though that made no sense it **REALLY** freaked Maisie out and she jumped inside one of her sleeping bags and said that she wouldn't come out because she didn't want to see the **"CREEPY WALL EARS"**.

Zach wouldn't stop packing the backpack and muttering things like "SHOULD HAVE KNOWN" and "IT'S ONLY A MATTER OF TIME" and Maisie was shaking SO BADLY I thought the whole tent might fall down!

But then Jodi put her fingers in her mouth and did her LOUD WHISTLE and everyone froze, even Maisie.

Then Jodi said, "ENOUGH! We have TRAINED for this, people. If this really IS a LEVEL ELEVEN EMERGENCY we know what to do. OK?"

But no one said anything so Jodi said,

"OK??!!"

We all nodded and said "CLEAR!" because we knew from our

LEVELS OF
EMERGENCY TRAINING

that Jodi had made us all do in her house after the time Zach got stuck in the bathroom for almost an hour because of the broken door handle, that we should shout "CLEAR!" in a situation like this.

Then Jodi said, "Bag?"

And Zach said, "CHECK!"

And then Jodi said, "Izzy. Pad?"

And I GRABBED a notepad and pen and said, "CHECK!"

And then Jodi said, "Maisie. JUMP!!"

And Maisie LEAPT out of her sleeping bag and on to Jodi's back.

And Jodi yelled, "GO! GO! GO! GO!"

The Meat Thing

As soon as we were in the woods Jodi shouted, **"SWITCH!"** and that meant it was someone else's turn to give Maisie a piggy-back because Jodi was getting tired. So Zach took Maisie and Jodi took the bag of LEVEL ELEVEN SUPPLIES and we ran through the woods until we found somewhere for the

SECRET MEETING.

Eventually Zach spotted a good place with a really big tree that looked good for sitting behind and keeping a LOOKOUT to make sure no one tried to SNEAK UP on us.

We quickly unpacked the backpack and COVERED Maisie in INSECT REPELLENT so we could have a

SECRET MEETING.

As soon as the meeting had OFFICIALLY BEGUN, Zach's eyes went HUGE.

Jodi said, "What is it? What's going on?"

Zach gulped a bit and said, "Izzy. Did the howling you heard sound a bit, um, HUMAN?"

I didn't really know what Zach meant but then he did a little howling noise and I realised that the howling HAD sounded a bit human.

Then Jodi said, "It wasn't howling Izzy heard. It was just the WIND!"

But I ignored Jodi because I knew that it WASN'T the wind that I'd heard and also because Zach was shaking his head, really slowly, backwards and forwards.

I could see by the look in Zach's eye that he KNEW what had made the howling sound and that it was BAD.

That's when Zach said, "I have to tell you. There is DANGER among us."

Jodi rolled her eyes because Zach was doing that THING he does when he makes EVERYTHING sound like a FILM and he won't just talk like a

NORMAL PERSON.

But then he said, "There's a

WEREWOLF

IN THE CAMP!"

Maisie GASPED and grabbed my hand so tight I YELPED.

Then Zach started talking about the WEIRD TREE SCRATCHES and how they had obviously been made by a WILD BEAST.

And he said that he couldn't stop thinking

about the GIANT POO and that it had
DEFINITELY looked a bit

WEREWOLF-Y.

And Maisie nodded loads.

Then Zach said, "And then there's the
MEAT THING."

Jodi looked at me and I looked at Jodi
because we both obviously had NO IDEA
what the MEAT THING was.

So that's when Zach explained that
SOMEONE AMONG US was OBSESSED
with eating MEAT and that that was a

CLEAR SIGN that they were a

WILD BEAST.

Maisie gasped and whispered, "MISS MOON!"

And Zach nodded and said, "It also explains her SUPER STRENGTH."

Then Maisie took FIVE DEEP BREATHS and said, "Miss Moon has really long nails. Mi-mi-maybe they're ... CLAWS!"

Zach's eyes went WIDE and he said that he thought Maisie was a hundred per cent CORRECT about the CLAWS. And that's when I remembered that Miss Moon had actually accidently scratched Jodi when she snatched the hammer out of her hand when we were putting up the tent.

Zach said that we also had to SERIOUSLY CONSIDER how TALL Miss Moon was because he did not think it was normal for a lady to be as tall as Miss Moon.

Zach explained that

are not like regular wolves because they are SHAPESHIFTERS. Zach said that when werewolves go into HUMAN FORM they would be much taller than everyone else because it would be like a huge wolf standing on its hind legs.

Then Jodi said that explained why Miss Moon had known all that stuff about the LAST WOLF IN SCOTLAND.

Zach said that he had SUSPECTED there was a

WEREWOLF AMONG US

the second I told him about the late-night HOWLING but that it was when he saw Miss Moon's HAIRY LEGS during the hot chocolate river game that he knew for sure.

And that's when we all looked at each other. And Maisie put her head in her hands

and said,

"NO. NO. NO.
NOT AGAIN.
NO. NO. NO."

And we all knew we had a SERIOUS PROBLEM.

Our PE teacher was a WEREWOLF.

WEREWOLF!

I couldn't BELIEVE that this was happening to us. I mean, we were living in a TENT in the middle of the WOODS with a WEREWOLF! Jodi was tapping her hands against her legs LOADS because that's what she does sometimes when she's a bit nervous.

And then she said, "Zach. Are we in DANGER?"

Zach took a DEEP BREATH and said that we were probably OK for now because Miss Moon was still in HUMAN FORM but that since she'd starting

HOWLING IN THE NIGHT

and growing HAIRY LEGS that it was probably just a MATTER OF TIME before she FULLY TRANSFORMED.

Jodi started tapping her legs LOADS when Zach said that and Maisie was looking a bit SWIRLY so that's when I took the pad and pen out of my jacket and started writing down everything that we knew about WEREWOLVES so we could make a plan about what to do next so we didn't get EATEN ALIVE!

Zach said that he was basically a WEREWOLF EXPERT which I was really pleased about because there wasn't a library at the campsite and phones and other devices were BANNED so we couldn't do research on the Internet. So we did the list

121

using only ZACH'S BRAIN:

WHAT WE KNOW ABOUT WEREWOLVES

1. Werewolves are in human form most of the time
2. A full moon makes them transform into wolf form
3. They are tall
4. Might have a long nose like a dog/wolf when in human form
5. They are obsessed with meat
6. Have super strength
7. Have long nails or claws
8. Totally hairy

Then Zach said that that was all he knew and that he was sorry he didn't know more.

Then Maisie said, "I might have broken the rules."

And she said it in such a tiny voice that I wasn't sure if I'd just imagined it or not until she reached into her pocket and pulled out her MOBILE PHONE!

Maisie made us all PINKY PROMISE that we wouldn't tell Miss Jones about her phone because she didn't want to be EXPELLED. She said that she'd sneaked her phone along with her on the trip because she was worried that a SNAKE or even a BEAR might get into our tent and that she'd need it to call

999.

But Maisie said that she didn't have any signal because of

THE WILDERNESS.

Zach said that if we could maybe just get a little bit of signal we could call the library and get them to read to us over the phone. But Jodi said she wasn't sure they did that but Maisie said that they DEFINITELY WOULD because we all have library cards.

But we couldn't get any phone signal at ALL, even when Zach pointed the phone at his own head (because he heard that your BRAIN WAVES can give your phone a signal).

Then Zach started waving the phone around until he shouted, "I've got TWO BARS!"

So we made Zach stand COMPLETELY STILL and tried to decide what to do next because we didn't actually know the number for the library. So that's when we decided we should text our friend AMY (who wasn't on the trip because of her tonsils) and ask her to look up stuff about werewolves and text it to us.

We couldn't decide what to say in the text until Zach said, "**HURRY UP!** It's gone down to **ONE BAR!**"

So we just quickly sent:

AMY.

WE NEED U TO TXT US EVERYTHING ABOUT WEREWOLVES ASAP!!

P.S. SORRY ABOUT BOTH OF YOUR TONSILS.

XXX

But as SOON as we pressed send we lost the signal, so we couldn't be sure if Amy got it or not.

But then Maisie said that she'd once read a poem about a werewolf and that it had said that werewolves were

SAD CREATURES

who didn't really like being werewolves and also that they were LONERS and that she was starting to feel bad for Miss Moon.

So we added LONER and SAD CREATURE to the list.

But then Jodi said that Miss Moon didn't seem very sad OR lonely and that she just seemed ANNOYED all the time.

And that's when we heard a noise.

A RUSTLING.

Then **TWIGS CRACKING**.

Maisie gasped so I put my hand over her mouth and stood with my back against the tree and Zach and Jodi hit the floor, just like Jodi had trained us to do.

I could hear the noise getting **CLOSER** and **CLOSER** and Maisie went limp so I knew that she had fainted. So I slowly slid down the tree until we were both lying on the ground next to Jodi and Zach.

And that's when we all saw it.

It was Miss Moon.

She was running through the forest!

She was running **SO FAST** that at first I was worried there might be something in the woods chasing her. But then I saw she was **GRINNING**. And she was even laughing a bit even though there was no one with her making her laugh or anything like that because she was **ALONE**.

We all held our breath as Miss Moon ran past us.

I looked at Maisie because I was hoping that she was still unconscious but she wasn't. Her eyes were WIDE OPEN and FROZEN IN FEAR.

We all lay completely still and didn't say a WORD until we couldn't see or hear Miss Moon any more.

The Missing Sausages

On our way back to the campsite Zach said that Miss Moon must **LOVE** running free in the forest because she is a **WILD ANIMAL**.

He said that we probably should have followed her and that if we had we might even have seen her **SCRATCHING** her

CLAWS against the trees.

As soon as we were out of the woods, I smelled the barbecue and I gasped and said, "It's the meat. She must've smelled the MEAT! That's why she was smiling and running so fast!"

Maisie agreed with me loads because she said that DOGS have a HEIGHTENED SENSE OF SMELL which means they can probably smell a cheeseburger from a mile away and that WOLVES and DOGS are sort of the same.

So we all hurried up to the campsite because we wanted to see if Miss Moon was there FEASTING and also because we were really hungry and the barbecue smelled good.

When we got there Miss Jones was cooking and Miss Moon was FIRST IN LINE with her paper plate, waiting for the burgers!

Miss Moon's face was BRIGHT RED from all the running and it even looked a bit like she was DROOLING!

We joined the back of the queue and watched Miss Moon CLOSELY as she asked for THREE BURGERS. She didn't even take a bun! She just sat down and ate all three burgers on their own, really fast.

When we got to the front of the queue I wasn't really that hungry for burgers any more because it was a bit disgusting watching Miss Moon scoff them like that.

So I asked for a sausage instead of a burger and that's when Miss Jones said the sausages were

MISSING!

Miss Jones let me have the halloumi cheese-and-tomato kebabs and a cheese roll, just like Jodi was having, because Jodi is a VEGETARIAN.

By the time we sat down Miss Moon had finished her MEAT FEAST and was going up for SECONDS.

That's when Jodi said, "She definitely IS obsessed with meat!"

And we all said that she DEFINITELY WAS.

Then we heard Miss Jones asking Miss Moon where she had been and if she knew where the MISSING SAUSAGES were.

We all leaned in as close as we could and my food nearly tipped off my plate because I was leaning forward so much.

THAT'S when Miss Moon's face went

EVEN MORE RED and she got a bit FLUSTERED and she said, "Erm, well, I'm sure they'll be in one of these cool boxes somewhere."

But she didn't even LOOK for them. She just grabbed another burger off the barbecue with her BARE HAND and wandered off with it.

That's when Zach said, "She knows fine well the sausages are gone. If they were here she'd be able to smell them a MILE AWAY. She's obviously stolen them and EATEN THEM RAW. That's probably what she was doing in the woods."

And we knew Zach was right.

Just then we heard loads of BEEPING coming from Maisie.

Then Zach said, "AMY! She must have got our TEXT!"

So Maisie took out her phone and her face went COMPLETELY PALE.

And that's because Amy had texted back:

WEREWOLVES ARE HUMANS WHO TRANSFORM INTO WOLF-LIKE CREATURES DURING A FULL MOON. FOLKLORE HAS IT THAT SOME WEREWOLVES CAN ALSO TRANSFORM WHEN THEY ARE ANGRY. A WEREWOLF IS LIKELY TO BECOME INCREASINGLY HAIRY PRIOR TO A FULL MOON. LOOK OUT FOR THE MEETING OF EYEBROWS (THE SO-CALLED "MONOBROW").

WILL SEND MORE LATER.

WHAT IS GOING ON THERE???!!!

That night, Zach said that it was time to take ACTION. And that meant we had to put our spending money together and buy loads of MEAT.

Zach said that if we HID meat near Miss Moon's tent then she would go WILD trying to find it and that she might even get SO ANGRY that she TRANSFORMED and we could take a video on Maisie's phone as EVIDENCE.

Zach said that if we caught Miss Moon in WEREWOLF FORM we could show it to Miss Jones and she would show it to the

POLICE and Miss Moon would get taken away and put in a WEREWOLF CAGE and we would be safe.

But then Maisie started crying because she said that it was not nice to keep human werewolves in a cage and that she still felt really sad about Miss Moon and her WEREWOLF DISEASE.

I hadn't thought about

WEREWOLFISM

being a disease before and I started to feel bad about the cage thing, too.

But then Zach told Maisie that it was OK and for her **OWN GOOD** because if she ate one of her pupils on a **FULL MOON** she would probably feel **TERRIBLE** and she'd also get sent to prison for life.

But that's when Jodi said, "If you're right, and Miss Moon **IS** a werewolf, we can't be sure she's a **NICE ONE**, Maisie. I mean, she's not a very **NICE** person as a human."

And that made Maisie gulp and she stopped crying right away.

We waited until everyone else was inside their tents getting ready for bed and then we put out our torches so that it looked as though we'd gone to bed and then we sat in the darkness for AGES so everyone thought we were asleep before sneaking out and down to the campsite shop.

The shop door made a BEEP BEEP sound when we opened it and we almost jumped out of our SKIN because we were on a SECRET MISSION so we were all a bit nervy.

It was SO BRIGHT inside the shop! Zach said hello to the shopkeeper and he gave us a bit of a weird look and Jodi told me to stop scrunching up my eyes so much because it was making us look suspicious (even though

I was a hundred per cent sure that the reason the shopkeeper was looking at us strangely was because Maisie was still wearing her SPACE SUIT SLEEPING BAG).

We hurried to the fridge at the back of the shop and looked to see what MEAT we could buy with our spending money.

Zach said that we should get loads of STEAK and BURY IT next to her tent and that that would drive her WILD. But we didn't have enough money for loads of steak so we bought four packs of 99p ham slices.

When we put all of our change on the counter to pay for the ham the shopkeeper shook his head and muttered "TEACHERS THESE DAYS" and "IT'S HEALTHY EATING GONE MAD" and "POOR SOULS" and then he put four bags of crisps and a packet of biscuits in the bag too and said "No charge."

I had no idea why we didn't have to pay and Zach said that if he'd known he would have got the steak. But Maisie said that the ham was BETTER because there were FIFTY SLICES in each packet so that meant we had

TWO HUNDRED SLICES.

We sneaked back up to camp and hid in the trees beside Miss Moon's tent.

That's when Zach said, "Right. Don't panic, Maisie, OK?"

And as SOON as Zach said that I just

KNEW that he wanted us to put the ham SUPER CLOSE to Miss Moon's tent. And that's EXACTLY what he DID want us to do!

Zach said that if we laid the slices of ham on the ROOF of her tent they would be DISGUISED because it was dark and Miss Jones wouldn't understand why the roof was smelling of meat and that would make her confused and hungry and ANGRY!

Maisie said, "NO WAY! It's too DANGEROUS!"

But then Zach said that Miss Moon would be fast asleep and that if we all helped we could do it really quickly and then run back into the trees and watch.

I thought this was

a REALLY bad idea

A really,

REALLY bad idea!

Because we all knew that werewolves had HEIGHTENED SENSES and that Miss Moon would probably wake up drooling within SECONDS!

But then Zach said that we had to take a BIG RISK if we wanted to catch her on camera.

So we told Maisie to wait in the trees but she said no and that she was too scared to be in the woods alone so we all went.

We each opened a packet of ham really quietly before we reached Miss Moon's tent and then we began laying out the ham slices and they sort of looked like pink roof tiles.

We did it AS FAST and as GENTLY as we could until the roof of the tent was completely covered. And then JUST as we were sneaking away we heard a rustling from inside the tent so we RAN!

Maisie was shaking like mad by the time we got back to our hiding spot and Zach must have been really scared too because he was trying to point Maisie's phone at Miss Moon's tent but it was shaking ALL OVER the place.

That's when Jodi said, "Give it to me." And she held it steady and ZOOMED IN on Miss Moon's tent.

We all huddled round Jodi and STARED at the screen. But nothing was happening.

That's when Maisie said, "I don't understand. We used two hundred slices!"

And Zach said, "We should have got the steak."

And Jodi said,

"SHHHHHHHH!"

But then we heard a **WEIRD WHIMPERING SOUND**. And Miss Moon's tent **UNZIPPING**.

And then we saw Miss Moon crawl out of her tent on **ALL FOURS!**

And there was hair **EVERYWHERE**.

And that's when we all gasped and Maisie fainted on top of Jodi and almost knocked her over and the phone fell into the mud.

And we ran.

Eyes in the Woods!

It took AGES to get back to our tent because we each had to carry Maisie by an arm or a leg and she felt a LOT heavier than usual because she'd put loads of TORCHES and BATTERIES and other stuff inside her sleeping bag.

As soon as we were back in our tent Jodi took out her mini-padlock and locked the door zips so we were safe.

We all said that Zach should DEFINITELY stay in our tent and that he could use one of Maisie's sleeping bags and sleep in the middle bit and he said OK and I knew that he would because he looked TERRIFIED.

Jodi wiped the mud off Maisie's phone and said that it wasn't broken so the VIDEO should still be on there. Maisie was still out cold but I put her eye mask on her JUST IN CASE she woke up while we were watching the video.

That's when Jodi said, "Are you ready?"

And then she pressed play before we could even answer.

It was too dark to see anything but after a few seconds we heard the WHIMPERING and TENT UNZIPPING.

And then we all

GASPED.

And Zach said, "Uuuuuum. Do you see that?!"

And we nodded that we did.

Because we could see

WEREWOLF EYES.

And Jodi said, "I don't think that person needs to worry about bringing wolves back to the wild.

They're already HERE."

Maisie didn't do OR say anything for AGES once we took off her eye mask and showed

her the

SHINING WEREWOLF EYES.

And then eventually she took a DEEP BREATH and said, "What next?"

But then Zach said, "Sssssssshhh!" because he thought he heard a noise outside so we all FROZE and Jodi turned the torch off and Maisie grabbed my hand and squeezed it so tight it made my EYES WATER.

We all sat in the dark, in silence, until Jodi eventually said, "Whatever it was, it's gone now."

And all of a sudden Maisie's phone BEEPED and we all SCREAMED!

Maisie's eyes went WIDE when she looked at the screen and then she said, "Are you ready?"

Maisie read out the message and it said:

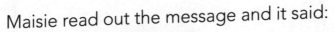

A BITE OR SCRATCH FROM A WEREWOLF WILL CAUSE THE AFFLICTION TO BE PASSED ON TO THE VICTIM.

P.S. ARE YOU ALL STILL ALIVE??

LOVE AMY XXX

Monobrow

We were all EXHAUSTED the next morning because NONE of us had managed to get ANY SLEEP because every time someone RUSTLED or COUGHED or SNORTED one of us would GASP and put the torch on to make sure a WEREWOLF hadn't sneaked into our tent.

It also didn't help that Maisie was OBSESSED with Amy's text about being able to PASS ON WEREWOLFISM and she kept touching her own arm hair and saying that it was getting LONGER and that it felt like WEREWOLF FUR.

At breakfast, we all sat really close together on one of the little picnic benches as we ate our cereal and looked around to see if Miss Moon was up yet.

But Miss Moon was NOWHERE to be seen. And Miss Jones was being grumpy about having to do all the TEACHER-Y stuff

like COUNT US ALL and make sure that we were all wearing Real Clothes (which was a new rule because Gary Petrie had tried to wear only pyjama bottoms and flip-flops the day before).

Then all of a sudden Maisie gasped and that's when we saw Miss Moon walking RIGHT TOWARDS US. And she did NOT look pleased.

That's when Zach started PANICKING, saying that she might have spotted us SPYING on her last night with her SUPER-SENSITIVE WEREWOLF EYES.

But Miss Moon walked past us and went

over to Miss Jones instead.

We all STARED at Miss Moon as she spoke to Miss Jones but the only word we managed to hear was BACON and then Miss Jones threw her arms in the air and said, "DO WHAT YOU WANT! I'm going to get changed!" and then she stormed off and I SWEAR Miss Moon did a low GROWLING SOUND.

I could feel Maisie edging closer and closer to me on the bench as Miss Moon sat down on the other side of our picnic table. She didn't even say hello, she just sat with her back to us so we couldn't see her face and drank her coffee in complete SILENCE.

Jodi pointed at Miss Moon's hair with a bit of a SHAKY FINGER and we all nodded LOADS because her hair looked CRAZY and there was NO WAY there'd been THAT much of it yesterday.

But then I felt Maisie begin to SLIP and before I could do anything she slid right off the bench and landed underneath the picnic table.

Miss Moon SLAMMED her coffee cup down and whipped her head around to face us and said, "What EXACTLY is WRONG with that child?"

But we couldn't really answer because we were too busy staring at her FACE. Her eyebrows were so HAIRY that they were almost TOUCHING in the middle!

And Zach gasped and said, "The so-called MONOBROW!"

Miss Moon NARROWED her eyes at him and said, "What did you just say?"

And that's when Zach realised that he had said it OUT LOUD so he just said, "Um … um… Nothing!" and picked up his spoon and pretended to be eating his cereal even though there wasn't any left in his bowl.

Miss Moon GROWLED a tiny bit and then

she got off her seat and CRAWLED UNDER THE PICNIC TABLE.

So we followed her and Jodi said, "She'll be fine. Come on, Maisie. Out you come."

Jodi started to drag Maisie out from under the picnic table. But then Miss Moon started HELPING and Maisie WOKE UP and saw Miss Moon and she took the deepest breath a person has ever taken and I knew EXACTLY what was about to happen and so did Jodi and Zach so we dropped Maisie and covered our ears and Maisie SCREAMED THE WHOLE FOREST DOWN.

Miss Moon looked FURIOUS and it was

probably because Maisie had screamed RIGHT in her EAR!

Miss Moon's face went RED and THAT'S when I remembered about a werewolf TRANSFORMING when it's ANGRY.

Zach had already begun to back out slowly

from under the table and he was pulling me with him. Then Miss Moon LEAPT out from under the table so fast I actually YELPED and she GRABBED her coffee mug and stormed away.

We all lay down on the grass next to the table because we were in SHOCK.

Jodi said that it was time to FACE FACTS and that Miss Moon was getting hairier by the day.

I said that she was also getting more and more ANGRY and everyone agreed.

Then Zach said, "You know what this means. It will soon be a FULL MOON."

Me and Jodi both gave Zach a LOOK when he said that last bit because Maisie was lying RIGHT THERE and Zach did his "OOPS" face that we do when we accidentally say stuff in front of Maisie that terrifies her to her very core.

So Zach asked Maisie if she was OK but Maisie didn't say anything and she had her head down so we couldn't see her face.

And when she looked up we saw that she was CRYING.

We all gave Maisie a hug and said that we would protect her from Miss Moon.

But then Maisie said, "But who will protect

Miss Moon from HERSELF?"

And that's when we realised that Maisie was crying because she was WORRIED about Miss Moon.

Then Maisie wiped her eyes and said, "We have to do something. We need to find a CURE!"

And that's when I got a

BRILLIANT IDEA!

Werewolves in Need

That afternoon, we all went to visitors' centre and when we got there I said, "I've got a plan. Follow me!"

My plan was to see if there was a COMPUTER we could use so we could find a WEREWOLF CURE. Jodi said that was a

BRILLIANT IDEA

and Maisie said we might even be able to find a charity for werewolves that could give us some advice on how to help them.

But we weren't allowed to use the computer in the visitors' centre because it said STAFF ONLY on it and also because it was behind the counter in the gift shop.

That's when Jodi said that this was an

EMERGENCY

and that sometimes you had to BREAK THE RULES when it was an emergency, like when it was about WEREWOLVES.

So we pretended to be looking around the EXHIBITION that was all about the JACOBITE SOLDIERS and a BATTLE that had happened. The plan was that Zach was going to cause a DIVERSION at the stationery bit by ACCIDENTALLY-ON-PURPOSE knocking ALL of the rubbers and pencils on to the ground.

Jodi said that would make the Gift Shop Man really annoyed and he would come over and moan at Zach a bit and start picking them all up while we sneaked behind the counter and used the computer.

But Zach said that this was probably the RISKIEST plan that Jodi had EVER come up with. And we knew he was right because the Gift Shop Man could come back at ANY TIME and catch us behind the counter and that he would probably call the POLICE!

But Maisie said that it HAD TO BE DONE and then she put her shaky little hand out in front of her.

I knew Maisie wanted us to all put our hands together for COURAGE because we were a TEAM just like we'd done when we thought there were BABY ALIENS in our school!

So we all put our hands on top of Maisie's and Jodi smiled a bit and said, "Werewolf Hunters," and Maisie said, "Werewolves in Need," and we all nodded and sent Zach off to wreck the stationery bit.

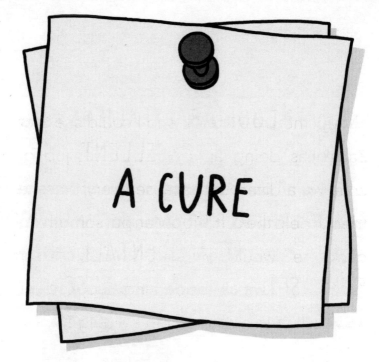

A CURE

As soon as Zach knocked over the tray with all the rubbers in it, the Gift Shop Man **RUSHED** over to see what was going on and we slid behind the counter.

Jodi opened a search page on the computer and wrote **"WEREWOLF CURE"**.

I was the LOOKOUT and I could see that Zach was doing an EXCELLENT job of creating a diversion because every time he tried to help the Gift Shop Man put something back he would ACCIDENTALLY-ON-PURPOSE knock something ELSE over and then say sorry and start helping to pick it all up.

But then the Gift Shop Man told Zach to "GO OVER THERE" and he pointed to the exhibition bit so Zach gave me the WARNING SIGN which was scratching his head with BOTH HANDS at the same time so I said, "It's time to GO!"

But then Jodi said that she'd "JUST PRESSED PRINT" and I started PANICKING because we hadn't said ANYTHING about using the PRINTER as well and I was SURE that we were going to get caught.

Me and Maisie RAN across to the printer while Jodi closed the search page and deleted the search history.

I almost had a

waiting for the page to finish printing. It felt

like EVERYTHING was going in SLOW MOTION and I could actually SEE the Gift Shop Man walking back over.

Then Maisie said, "DONE!" and snatched the bit of paper from the printer and we slipped around the side of the counter JUST before the Gift Shop Man came back.

We all sat on the ground for AGES trying to calm down because that had been a CLOSE ONE.

Then we spotted Zach WAVING at us. So we ran back over to the exhibition bit and that's when we all looked at the piece of paper. And this is what it said:

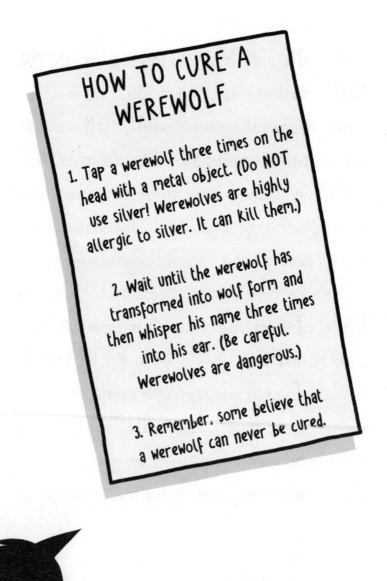

HOW TO CURE A WEREWOLF

1. Tap a werewolf three times on the head with a metal object. (Do NOT use silver! Werewolves are highly allergic to silver. It can kill them.)

2. Wait until the werewolf has transformed into wolf form and then whisper his name three times into his ear. (Be careful. Werewolves are dangerous.)

3. Remember, some believe that a werewolf can never be cured.

NO ONE wanted to do the WHISPERING ONE and that was fair enough.

Maisie said that the METAL ONE didn't say that the werewolf had to be in WOLF FORM when you did the tapping and that we could try it on Miss Moon at breakfast the next day when she was eating her cereal.

Then Zach pointed to a poster about the BATTLE and said that if it happened here then it had probably been a WEREWOLF BATTLE. He said that some of the werewolves must have SURVIVED the battle and managed to get away.

Zach said that everything made sense to

him now especially about why Miss Moon had suggested we all go on a CAMPING TRIP.

He said that this place was basically like an all-inclusive holiday camp for werewolves because there were woods to roam in, other werewolves to meet, trees to scratch, fresh running water to drink from the river and campers to FEAST ON!

Then Zach said that we had to be EXTRA CAREFUL because we were on

WEREWOLF TERRITORY

and that when the FULL MOON came Miss Moon would FULLY TRANSFORM and become a hungry, DANGEROUS BEAST.

And Maisie gulped.

★

That night, we all gathered around the campfire and toasted marshmallows.

Miss Moon was EVEN HAIRIER than she'd been this morning and her eyebrows were actually TOUCHING.

And then all of a sudden Jodi said, "I have to go to bed. I'm too tired." And she left even though she had LOADS of marshmallows left.

Zach said, "That's weird."

And it WAS weird because Jodi

LOVES toasted marshmallows.

Then when we all went back to our tent Jodi wasn't THERE!

I was just about to start

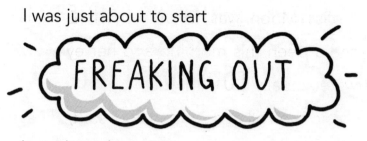

when I heard snoring.

It was coming from Zach's SURVIVAL TENT and when we peeked inside we saw that Jodi was in there fast asleep.

I had no idea why Jodi had gone to sleep in Zach's tent but then Maisie said that maybe she was feeling sick from all the marshmallows so we just zipped the tent back up and went to bed.

But later that night I woke up suddenly

because I thought I heard

outside our tent.

I held my breath to see if I could hear it again but there was nothing.

So I just lay there trying to decide what to do next and I must have fallen asleep because then it was morning and Zach was shaking me awake, shouting,

The Full Moon Mission

I couldn't BELIEVE that Jodi was gone and I just KNEW that we should NEVER have let her sleep in the SURVIVAL TENT by herself when we knew FINE WELL there was a WEREWOLF in the camp.

We all ran outside and started asking

everyone if they'd seen Jodi and Maisie was crying because she thought Miss Moon had eaten her and then all of a sudden a voice said, "What's going on?!"

And it was JODI!

We all HUGGED Jodi SO TIGHT she said, "STOP ... CAN'T ... BREATHE." So we stopped.

Jodi said that she'd just gone to the shower block and that we all needed to

and that she was a hundred per cent fine.

But she didn't LOOK a hundred per cent fine. She had big dark circles under her eyes and her face was all red and blotchy.

That's when I noticed that Jodi had a HUGE backpack with her and when I asked her why she'd taken so much stuff to the showers she just said, "Um... LISTEN! We have a new mission. We need to find out when the next full moon is! So we can be READY."

Then all of a sudden a DARK SHADOW covered Jodi and we turned around to see Miss Moon HOVERING over us.

I gulped because Miss Moon looked HAIRIER than ever. Her hair was ALL OVER the place and she even had a bit of a MOUSTACHE now.

Miss Moon STARED AT US for ages.

She looked angry.

Then she said, "You're LATE for breakfast. HURRY UP!" and stormed off.

But we all knew that this was NO TIME for breakfast. We needed to start the Full Moon Mission RIGHT AWAY because Miss Moon was now SO HAIRY that we knew the full moon must be REALLY SOON.

And we all knew that if the full moon happened while we were camping we would be in GRAVE DANGER.

So we quickly grabbed some SUPPLIES and sneaked off into the woods to our den.

It wasn't long before we had to admit that we were a hundred per cent LOST.

Jodi tried to say that we WEREN'T lost and that her SHORT CUT had WORKED but I said I didn't think ending up COMPLETELY LOST meant that a short cut had worked.

But then Jodi started getting really ANGRY at me and saying that she had a COMPASS and also that she knew EXACTLY what she was doing.

So I got angry back and said that watching

"EXTREME SURVIVAL"

didn't make her an

ACTUAL SURVIVAL EXPERT.

Jodi got SO ANGRY when I said that that her face went RED and she stormed off into the woods by herself.

So Zach ran after her because he said that the LAST thing we should do was split up.

I sat down on the ground with Maisie and she gave me a snack from the bag.

When Jodi and Zack came back Jodi said that her compass was OBVIOUSLY BROKEN because North should stay in the same place and that the dial shouldn't spin around all over the place when you are actually standing still.

That's when Zach said that it was a bit **SPOOKY** how much the **COMPASS DIAL** was **SPINNING** and that maybe it had something to do with the **FULL MOON** and

WEREWOLF ENERGY.

And Maisie gulped and started measuring the length of her ARM HAIRS again with a ruler because she was still scared about catching the WEREWOLF AFFLICTION.

Jodi put the compass back in her bag and took a deep breath and said, "OK. I have a confession."

We all STARED at Jodi.

And Jodi said,

"I'm LOST."

Lost in the Wilderness

Maisie started to shake a bit when Jodi said that because it's a bit scary when the only

SURVIVAL EXPERT

in your group actually says that you're lost.

Maisie took her phone out but she didn't have any signal so we knew we couldn't phone the army or anything like that.

So we all sat quietly because Jodi said that she needed SILENCE so she could THINK and get CONNECTED TO NATURE.

Then all of a sudden Jodi's eyes

SNAPPED OPEN

and she said, "Right. I can DO THIS!"

And that's when we all thought Jodi had gone a bit MAD because she started digging up mud and SMEARING it all over her FACE.

We sat **STARING** at Jodi with our mouths **WIDE OPEN**. But then Jodi said, "CAMOUFLAGE!"

Jodi said that we had **NO IDEA** what might be **LURKING** in the woods and that

we had to use CAMOUFLAGE to protect ourselves from PREDATORS. And before Jodi had even finished her sentence Maisie had COVERED herself in mud.

Jodi gave Maisie a SALUTE and said that our NUMBER ONE PRIORITY was SHELTER because WHO KNEW how long we'd be lost in the woods before someone found us or we managed to find our way out.

I started to get REALLY SCARED because I DEFINITELY didn't want to spend the night in the woods so I said that maybe we should just try to get out and if we couldn't we could make a shelter then.

But Jodi said that that was the NUMBER ONE mistake that people made in Season One of "EXTREME SURVIVAL" because by the time it gets dark it's TOO LATE to find the materials you need to build your shelter and then you lose.

Then Jodi's eyes went REALLY WIDE and she looked TOTALLY SCARY because of all the mud on her face.

And she said, "And this is not a GAME. This is REAL LIFE. So if you don't have a shelter by nightfall you don't lose out here, you..."

But Jodi didn't finish her sentence because

Maisie was SHAKING.

But we all knew what the last word was and none of us wanted to die OR get eaten by werewolves so we started looking for things to build a shelter with.

We collected all the branches and leaves we could find and tried to make a roof thing over the two big branches that were sticking out from an old tree and it actually looked quite good by the time we were finished.

We lay down under the roof and looked up to see if there were any holes in case it rained. And then we poked our fingers through the holes so Jodi knew where to put the leaves and twigs to make it as WATERTIGHT as possible.

Then Jodi said that our next PRIORITY was WARMTH and then she started unpacking her backpack and I saw that she had brought ALL of her clothes!

I didn't know why Jodi had done that but I was glad that she had because I definitely didn't want to freeze to death if someone didn't find us before nightfall.

So we all put Jodi's clothes on top of what we were already wearing and Zach didn't even complain when Jodi gave him a pink jumper with a KOALA on it because he

knew that this was about

SURVIVAL.

Then Jodi said that when night came it was going to get colder and colder and she was going to build a FIRE.

Zach said that he didn't think rubbing two sticks together was going to help and that we needed some FUEL. But then Jodi said that she had SEEN IT ON TV WITH HER OWN EYES and Zach couldn't really say anything after that because we all knew that Jodi had been a hundred per cent right about everything so far. And we also knew that if Jodi hadn't watched "EXTREME SURVIVAL" that we'd all probably be

WEREWOLF MEAT

by now.

So we all sat and ate the snacks Maisie had packed and watched as Jodi rubbed two sticks together for AGES. But nothing happened.

So that's when Jodi said that FIRE was no longer the next priority and that WATER was the next priority instead.

Then Jodi got a BIG SMILE on her face and went into her bag and brought out a SURVIVAL STRAW. Jodi said that she'd bought it on eBay and that you could drink water from ANYWHERE using it, even a PUDDLE, and that the straw made it taste just like normal water from the tap and kept all the BACTERIA and INSECTS and DISEASES out.

I was just about to say there was NO WAY I was drinking from a PUDDLE when Maisie's backpack BEEPED.

We all SCREAMED because we knew that it meant that Maisie had a PHONE SIGNAL and that meant we could call for HELP!

Maisie THREW her phone at Zach because she was PANICKING a bit and because the phone only had ONE BAR of reception. Zack looked at the phone and said that there was a new message from Amy. And then he stopped smiling.

We all
rushed over
to look at the
message.
It said:

FULL MOON ON
FRIDAY.

BE CAREFUL!!

AMY

XXX

And we all gasped.

Because TODAY was FRIDAY!!

Zach said that Amy must have sent the
text the day before but that we didn't get it
because we didn't have a phone signal until
now.

Then Maisie said, "Amy was trying to warn us. And now we're stuck in the WOODS on a FULL MOON!"

Then Jodi jumped up and yelled, "QUICK! CALL FOR HELP WHILE WE CAN!"

So Zach tried to phone his mum but then he said, "NO!!" because we lost the signal again.

Then Maisie yelled, "999!" and we all looked at her and she said that even if you had NO SIGNAL you could still dial the EMERGENCY SERVICES and you might get through!

So Jodi grabbed the phone from Zach

and started to dial **999** and that's when the battery died and Jodi SCREAMED,
"NOOOOOOOOOOOOOOOOO!"

The Full Moon

After the **PHONE DISASTER** Maisie started writing a letter to her mum telling her how much she loved her and how she wanted to donate all her belongings to

WEREWOLVES IN NEED.

That's when Zach said we should use the SHERBET DIPS to send up a SMOKE SIGNAL.

So we emptied the sherbet on to our hands and started THROWING it into the air. But it didn't reach very high and then Jodi said to STOP because we were wasting VALUABLE FOOD RESOURCES and WHO KNEW how long we were going to be

LOST IN THE WILDERNESS.

Even though it was only one o'clock in the afternoon, Jodi said that we should all get some rest so that we had the ENERGY to find our way out of the woods the next morning and that she would take the FIRST WATCH while we slept.

So me, Zach and Maisie all lay down on the ground and put more of Jodi's clothes from her bag over us like a blanket while Jodi kept an eye out for PREDATORS (which we all knew meant WEREWOLVES).

I wasn't sleepy AT ALL but I must have fallen asleep at one point because when I woke up I heard WHIMPERING and a little bit of HOWLING!

Maisie was fast asleep and so was Zach so I sat up SLOWLY and very QUIETLY and peeked outside.

That's when I saw Jodi sitting in the woods on a rock.

The noise stopped and Jodi started to turn her head so I lay back down as fast as I could and shut my eyes and stayed COMPLETELY STILL.

My mind was RACING because I knew that

the **WHIMPERING** and **HOWLING** sounds had been coming from Jodi! And that they were the **SAME SOUNDS** I'd heard that night in my tent!

And that's when I remembered Amy's text about how a **SCRATCH** from a **WEREWOLF** can give you **WEREWOLFISM**.

I reached over and gently took the ruler out of Maisie's hand because I knew Maisie didn't need to worry about measuring her arm hairs.

But Jodi did!

I had **NO IDEA IN THE WORLD** what I was supposed to do next. I mean, my **BEST FRIEND** was turning into a

WEREWOLF!!

215

I lay there trying not to panic and I kept thinking over and over about how Miss Moon had SCRATCHED JODI'S HAND by accident when we were putting our tent up. And how Jodi had been acting a bit WEIRD lately, like when she went to bed EARLY even though she had

LOADS

of marshmallows left and when she disappeared off to the shower block with ALL of her clothes.

That's when I knew. She was going through

WEREWOLF TRANSFORMATION.

And that was why she wanted to sleep on her own in Zach's tent last night. In case she woke up all hairy!

I was just about to wake the others and tell them we had to find a spoon when I heard the sound of BRANCHES SNAPPING outside.

I sat up just a TINY bit so I could peek out of the shelter and that's when I saw her.

It was Miss Moon!

We're all
WEREWOLF
MEAT!

Before I could even SCREAM, Miss Moon told us to come with her "RIGHT AWAY" and also to "WIPE THAT MUD OFF YOUR FACES!"

So we grabbed our bags and followed Miss Moon into the woods because even though she was a werewolf she was still a teacher when she was in HUMAN FORM so we didn't really have a choice.

Miss Moon moved REALLY QUICKLY through the woods so we had to run a bit to keep up with her.

I looked over at Jodi and she looked

MEGA WEIRD.

I wanted to tell her it was OK and that she would ALWAYS be my BEST FRIEND even if we couldn't cure her but I didn't want to say anything in front of Miss Moon. So I just linked my arm through Jodi's and held her really close as we followed Miss Moon back to camp and when Jodi wasn't looking I took the ruler out of my pocket and tried to measure her arm hairs.

But then Jodi CAUGHT ME with the ruler and she pulled her arm away and said, "What are you DOING?"

So I said, "Nothing!" but it came out all high and squeaky because it is really hard to make your voice sound normal when you've just found out that your best friend is a werewolf!

And that's when I spotted something.

Jodi wasn't wearing her locket.

The locket that she ALWAYS wears that has a picture of her mum in it.

Her SILVER locket!

As soon as we got back to camp, Miss Moon took Jodi away somewhere and that was my CHANCE.

I pulled Zach and Maisie into the Big Tent and told them about Jodi being a

WEREWOLF!

Maisie and Zach were SHOCKED and Zach even had to lie down a bit because he said his head was SPINNING.

Zach said that explained why Jodi hadn't wanted to do the WEREWOLF INVESTIGATION in the first place and why she kept saying that I had just IMAGINED the howling, because she didn't want us to know that the howling had come from HER.

Maisie said that Jodi must have been trying to RUN AWAY that morning when we caught her with her backpack and that was why she had all her clothes with her.

Then I told Zach and Maisie about the SILVER LOCKET and how Jodi wasn't wearing it, even though she ALWAYS wears it, and one time she even said that she would probably DIE if she ever lost it because she loved it so much and that it used to be her GREAT-GRAN'S.

Maisie started crying and saying "POOR JODI" over and over again and saying that Jodi must be worried that we wouldn't want to be her friends any more and that she must be TOO SCARED to tell us.

And that made me cry a bit too because I didn't want Jodi to think that we didn't want to be her friends because we would ALWAYS be her friends, no matter ANYTHING EVER!

But then Zach said that we needed to

PULL OURSELVES TOGETHER

and make a plan, because that's what Jodi would want us to do if she were here.

But Zach got tears in his eyes when he said it and that nearly made me start crying again but I managed to be **STRONG** because we had to help our Werewolf Friend.

So we made a plan. And this is what we came up with:

1. Find Jodi and make sure she knows we are still her best friends even though she is a werewolf now.
2. Tap her on the head with a spoon.
3. If that doesn't work, make sure she stays in the tent during the full moon so she doesn't eat us.
4. Make a hole in the tent and stick a survival straw through and try to whisper Jodi's name in her werewolf-y ear three times.
5. Let her out after the full moon and give her lots of hugs and ALL of the snacks Maisie brought.

Then just as we were about to go looking for Jodi, Maisie's backpack started BEEPING.

Maisie looked a bit surprised and then she said, "My phone ran out of battery when Jodi was trying to dial 999. But now it says it's got 75% battery left!"

Then Zach gasped and explained that Jodi must have just PRETENDED that the phone battery had died because she didn't want us to call 999 in case the police found out she was a werewolf and took her away to be experimented on because werewolves are very RARE.

But then Zach stopped talking.

An Unexpected Guest

The zip on our tent started to SLOWLY move up and Maisie actually LEAPT on to my knee so I couldn't even MOVE to do something because Maisie was pinning me down!

Zach rushed forward and pulled the zip

back down and put the little suitcase lock on.

But then the voice said, "It is I. The River King!"

Zach looked at me and I didn't know what else to do so I just nodded at him and he let Gary Petrie in.

Gary came in and looked around at our living room bit and then he sat down and said, "Nice tent. It's not soundproofed, though."

That's when we realised that Gary Petrie had been LISTENING outside and that he had probably heard EVERYTHING.

Gary took a Twix and started eating it.

Then he said, "It sounds like you need help."

So I said, **"NO THANK YOU"** and then I took the second half of the Twix out of his hand because it wasn't his and he hadn't even ASKED if he could have it!

But Gary just smiled and said, "I know about JODI."

I was just about to tell Gary Petrie to GO AWAY when Maisie said, "Go on."

And that's when Gary said that he KNEW something was up because when he had been checking that everything was in order at the River Garry sign this morning and giving it a polish he had noticed Jodi in the phone box making **WEIRD NOISES.**

And that's when Maisie said, "We're worried that Jodi might be, um, well, a

WEREWOLF.

Do you have the power to help with that, Gary?"

And Gary stood up and put his hands on his hips and said, **"I HAVE THE POWER!"**

Me and Zach both **GASPED** and said, **"MAISIE!"** because we didn't think we should tell people about Jodi when it was

up to us to

PROTECT HER WEREWOLF SECRET!

But Maisie said that it was OK and that Gary wouldn't tell anyone and that she TRUSTED HIM.

Gary smiled LOADS when Maisie said that and I could see that he had obviously just eaten a whole bag of cheese puffs before he came to see us.

I was a bit in SHOCK because I had

NO IDEA that Maisie TRUSTED GARY PETRIE but then I remembered about how he had saved her from the FAKE HOT CHOCOLATE RIVER and realised that THAT must have been when she started trusting him.

Gary Petrie pointed his pinky finger at Maisie, but Gary Petrie usually has BOGEY FINGERS so I didn't think Maisie would do the Pinky Promise, but she did. And then Maisie and Gary both said "PROMISE!" at exactly the same time and started giggling.

Then Gary said that he was very sorry Jodi was a werewolf and Maisie said thank you.

Then before we could stop her, Maisie told Gary Petrie all about Miss Moon, too!

And after Gary had heard everything about the **CLAWS** and the **MEAT OBSESSION** and the **SO-CALLED MONOBROW** he said that it sounded like Miss Moon had turned Jodi into a werewolf on **PURPOSE** and that she was the **ALPHA WEREWOLF**.

And even though we had

NO IDEA

what that meant we knew that it was going to be **BAD**.

The
Alpha
Werewolf

As soon as Gary Petrie told us what an ALPHA WEREWOLF was we all RUSHED OUT of the tent to find Jodi. Because Gary Petrie said that an ALPHA WEREWOLF is the werewolf that CONTROLS other werewolves and that he'd seen it on TV so it

was definitely true. And that Miss Moon was probably using her ALPHA WEREWOLF POWERS to

BRAINWASH

Jodi into eating us alive!

But we couldn't find Jodi OR Miss Moon ANYWHERE!

That's when Maisie said that this was TOO SERIOUS and that we needed to tell Miss Jones what was going on RIGHT NOW and we all agreed.

So we all went over to where Miss Jones

was getting stuff ready for dinner and told her that we had a SERIOUS PROBLEM and that it was about JODI.

That's when Miss Jones put down the barbecue tongs and said that she knew all about Jodi and her PROBLEM and that Jodi was having a nap in Miss Jones's tent and that we shouldn't disturb her because she was EXHAUSTED.

Then Miss Moon appeared out of NOWHERE and said, "Actually, I'm feeling quite exhausted myself. I'm going to go for a lie-down in my tent while you cook dinner, Miss Jones." And then she left.

Miss Jones looked FURIOUS and before we could ask her any more questions about Jodi she STORMED off.

That's when Maisie said that she had never SEEN Miss Jones as mad as that before and that it must be because she was very ANGRY at Miss Moon for turning Jodi into a WEREWOLF.

Even though Miss Jones had said not to disturb Jodi, Maisie said that we knew a LOT more about werewolves than Miss Jones did because she was new to this whole WEREWOLF THING and that she probably didn't even REALISE that it was

almost a FULL MOON. So we sneaked

over to Miss Jones's tent and peeked inside.

But Jodi was GONE!

It was hard not to PANIC when we realised

Jodi was ON THE LOOSE but we knew

that we had to

and THINK so that we could find her and

stop her from doing something she didn't

mean to, like eat a rabbit. Because that would

be HORRIBLE because Jodi is actually a

vegetarian.

Zach said that Jodi might be having a

PRE-FULL MOON
WEREWOLF MEETING

with Miss Moon, so we all RAN over to Miss Moon's tent but her tent was WIDE OPEN and there was NO ONE inside, even though Miss Moon had JUST SAID that she was going for a nap.

Maisie started to panic because she said that Jodi could be ANYWHERE and then she started shaking LOADS and her eyes went all SWIRLY.

But then Gary Petrie picked up Maisie and put her over his shoulder and said, "FOLLOW ME!!" and started running down towards the river.

So we ran after them and that's when I realised that Gary was taking us to the PHONE BOX!

And that's when we found her.

Jodi was INSIDE THE PHONE BOX!

But then Zach suddenly PUSHED us all into the bushes and said, "SSSSSSSSSHHHHHHHH, Gary!" because Gary was still shouting stuff about the river and waving a stick around like a sword.

Zach said that we couldn't let Jodi SEE US because then she might RUN and then we'd lose her again. He said that we should try to keep Jodi in the phone box because she wouldn't be able to use her WEREWOLF CLAWS to SCRATCH her way out of there and that we could try to WHISPER HER NAME into her ear using the SURVIVAL STRAW.

Maisie said that she thought Jodi was in the phone box because she was speaking to a WEREWOLF HELPLINE and that they were probably trying to keep her CALM and ALREADY whispering her name into her ear to try to stop the FULL TRANSFORMATION.

But Gary Petrie said that Jodi had probably gone into the phone box to TRANSFORM, like Superman, and that she might be able to use her

SUPER WEREWOLF STRENGTH

to break the glass and ESCAPE.

Maisie pulled her BINOCULARS out of her backpack and when we looked through them we saw that Jodi's face was now covered in LONG HAIR.

Then Jodi started shaking her head ALL OVER THE PLACE and that's when we got a peek of her face and it was SERIOUSLY RED and BLOTCHY.

That's when we knew that, even though it wasn't actually dark yet, Jodi's transformation had BEGUN.

Our Best Werewolf

So we made a plan. The plan was that Gary Petrie would keep the door shut so Jodi couldn't ESCAPE and eat a rabbit while Maisie sang a SOOTHING SONG and me and Zach tried to whisper her name into her WEREWOLF EAR and CURE HER.

Then Maisie took a **SPOON** out of her pocket and said that we should also try to tap Jodi's head **THREE TIMES** if we got a chance.

Gary Petrie looked at us all like we were a bit **MAD** but that was because he didn't know all about **WEREWOLF CURES** like we did. So we told him that there wasn't time to explain and that we just needed him to hold the door shut.

Gary said that was **"TOO EASY"** and **"A WASTE OF HIS POWERS"** but that he would do it anyway.

And then all of a sudden Zach yelled, **"GO!"**

So we ran.

☆

We all CHARGED towards the phone box and Gary held the door shut and Maisie started singing at the TOP OF HER LUNGS.

Then I shouted through the glass to Jodi that we were going to SAVE her and that she was our BEST FRIEND and that we actually LOVED her but Jodi didn't say anything back; she just stood there covering her face with her hands so that we couldn't see her WEREWOLF FUR or SO-CALLED MONOBROW.

Then I noticed that Zach was trying to say

something to me. But I couldn't hear him because Maisie's **SOOTHING SONG** was actually **MEGA LOUD** (and not really very soothing).

So Zach pointed at the straw and pointed to the door and that was when I realised that the only way we were going to get the straw into the phone box was to open the door a little. So we told Gary Petrie to open the door just a TINY BIT so we could slip the straw through and position it next to Jodi's ear.

But as SOON as Gary opened the door just a crack Jodi started PUSHING at it and making loads of weird

HOWLING SOUNDS!

And Gary said,

"I ... CAN'T ... HOLD ... IT!
SHE'S ... TOO ...
STRONG! ARRRRGGGGGGH!"

And then before I realised what was happening Gary let go of the door and Jodi ESCAPED!

And as I watched Jodi run towards the woods, I thought that it might be the last time I was EVER going to see my best friend and that we would LOSE HER in the WILDERNESS for ever!

But then Zach GRABBED the sleeping bag Maisie had attached to her backpack and RAN after Jodi AS FAST as he could and we all followed.

Jodi wasn't running as fast as she usually does because she was still trying to cover her face so Zach managed to catch up with her and then he threw the sleeping bag over her to stop her running away.

Then me and Zach GRABBED Jodi and started carrying her back to camp and Maisie said, "Don't worry, Jodi. We're trying to HELP you. The sleeping bag is so you don't SCRATCH anyone. It's for your own good.

We know that you're a WEREWOLF."

And THAT'S when Jodi started shaking and wriggling like MAD and Gary Petrie started SCREAMING, "THIS IS IT!" and that when we took the sleeping bag off Jodi she would be

"A COMPLETE WEREWOLF!"

But then we heard Jodi say, "WHAT? No, I WON'T!"

And then Jodi started LAUGHING HYSTERICALLY and it was REALLY hard to carry her because she was jiggling ALL OVER THE PLACE so we had to put her down.

Zach said what we were WITNESSING was the effect of the FULL MOON and that the moon was starting to drive Jodi to MADNESS.

That was when Jodi sat up and showed us her face and there was NO HAIR (even though it WAS red and blotchy).

And she said, "What's **WRONG** with you all? I'm not a **WEREWOLF!**" and she could **BARELY** get her words out because she was laughing so hard.

So we explained about how Miss Moon had **SCRATCHED HER** and how she'd gone a bit **WEIRD** after that and went to bed early without eating all her marshmallows and then slept in Zach's tent by herself and kept disappearing off to the phone box and **LYING** about where she was going.

And Jodi stood up and went all **CALM** and said, "**DO I LOOK** like a werewolf?"

And we all said no because her hair wasn't

in her face any more and she seemed really calm now (even though her face was STILL a bit red and blotchy).

So that's when I asked Jodi why she had been HIDING HER FACE FROM US and why her face was all RED and BLOTCHY and also why she wasn't wearing her SILVER LOCKET that she ALWAYS wears.

And THAT'S when Jodi went REALLY WEIRD and her face started TREMBLING and she started to making a GRUNTING SOUND and then before I knew what was happening she was HOWLING!!

And THAT'S when we realised what was

happening.

Jodi was just CRYING.

I mean, REALLY crying. And I realised that I'd never seen Jodi cry before. EVER! (And also that she was really, really TERRIBLE at it!)

Zach and Maisie looked

SHOCKED

and then eventually I said, "Jodi, are you CRYING?"

And Jodi said, "GRRRRSSS YAAASS! I AAAAAAM!"

So we all stepped SLOWLY towards Jodi and hugged her a bit and asked her what was wrong and also if she was in any PHYSICAL PAIN because she sounded a bit like a WOUNDED BEAST.

That's when Jodi told us EVERYTHING. She said that it was HER CRYING that I'd thought was HOWLING on the first night and that she had tried to hide it from everyone by going to sleep in Zach's tent.

So we patted Jodi's back and Maisie stroked her hair and we told her that she was our BEST FRIEND and that everything was going to be OK.

Then Maisie said, "But what are you crying about, Jodi?"

Jodi looked like she didn't want to tell us.

But then she took a deep breath and said, "Because I'm **HOMESICK** and I miss my **MUUUUUUUUUUUM** and I lost my locket and I've been trying to phone my mum to hear her voice but every time I come down to use the phone box my mum doesn't answer and I-I-I **JUST WANT MY MUUUUUUUUUUUUM!**"

And I was

SHOCKED

because I had **NEVER** seen Jodi get **HOMESICKNESS** before and I felt **REALLY BAD** for her.

Jodi said that she'd been **SO HOMESICK** that morning that she'd packed all of her stuff and taken it with her to the phone box and tried to phone her mum to ask her to come and take her home.

Maisie said, "Why didn't you just **TELL US** about losing your locket and being homesick? We could have helped you find it."

But Jodi said that she didn't want us to think that she was a **BIG BABY** because

SHE was meant to be a SURVIVAL EXPERT and survival experts aren't meant to get HOMESICK and that she was meant to be the BRAVE ONE and that she was EMBARRASSED about being homesick.

Then Jodi started sobbing again and saying that her special locket was GONE FOR GOOD and that she'd already tried looking for it and it was

NOWHERE TO BE FOUND.

So we all sat on the ground and hugged Jodi for ages and Maisie gave her a tissue from her sleeve and some Maltesers that she had in her pocket.

Then Zach asked Jodi why she had pretended Maisie's phone battery was dead when we were lost in the wilderness. And Jodi said that she hadn't and that she must have switched the phone off by accident when she was trying to phone 999 because of all the PANIC.

When Jodi eventually calmed down her face was all red and blotchy from crying and her hair was hanging all over her face and she looked just like she had earlier when we'd seen her in phone box.

Jodi wiped her face and fixed her hair and said, "OK. I'm OK. "

And then she stood up and said, "Right. We need to FOCUS."

And I wasn't sure exactly what Jodi wanted us to focus on until she said, "We still have the small problem of Miss Moon being a WEREWOLF!"

And that's when we heard the

SCREAMING.

The Return of the Missing Sausages!

When we got to camp we were a hundred per cent **PREPARED** to come face-to-face with Miss Moon in **WOLF FORM**.

But we didn't. We came face-to-face with Miss Moon in **HUMAN FORM** wearing her **DRESSING GOWN!**

We all stood with our mouths WIDE OPEN because Miss Moon looked TERRIFIED and she was running around in circles SQUEALING at the top of her LUNGS and Miss Jones was trying to get her to STOP and we had NO IDEA what was going on!

Miss Moon stopped running and jumped up on to one of the picnic benches and that was when Zach said, "Does Miss Moon look a bit different to you?"

So we all looked more closely and THAT'S when we saw that Miss Moon DID look different! Her hair was all straight and shiny and her legs weren't hairy at ALL and her

monobrow had completely DISAPPEARED!

Then all of a sudden Miss Moon screamed, **"THERE THEY ARE! THE WILD BEASTS! LOOK!"** and she pointed a shaky finger at one of the **CARAVANS** behind all of our tents. And that's when we saw two huge **FOXES** pulling a string of sausages out of a caravan and into the woods.

Then Miss Moon started **SCREAMING**, "Those **WILD BEASTS** have been **TERRORISING** me since I got here! They crawled **ALL OVER** my tent one night and I didn't get **A WINK** of sleep. And **NOW** they've **INVADED** my caravan and stolen all of my **SAUSAGES!!**"

And **THAT'S** when Miss Jones's face went **RED** and she shouted, "**EXCUSE ME,** Miss **MOON!** But what do you mean **YOUR CARAVAN?!**"

Miss Moon's face went **BRIGHT RED**, too, and that's when Jodi shouted, "**GET BACK EVERYONE!** Miss Moon is about transform into a **WEREWOLF!!**"

So we all ducked under one of the picnic tables and waited.

But nothing happened.

And then Miss Jones said, "What on EARTH is going on?!"

⭐

Miss Jones made us all come out from under the picnic table and then she asked us why Jodi had called Miss Moon a werewolf and why Maisie wouldn't open her eyes and why Gary Petrie was hiding inside a sleeping bag!

So that's when we told Miss Jones about Miss Moon's SUPER STRENGTH and her MEAT OBSESSION and the GLOWING WEREWOLF EYES that we'd seen when we did the HAM PLAN.

Miss Jones listened carefully, and she even made us repeat some bits, like the bits about Miss Moon being GRUMPY and having a MONOBROW.

Miss Jones said that she was CERTAIN that Miss Moon WASN'T a werewolf but she agreed that Miss Moon had some explaining to do and then she crossed her arms and STARED at Miss Moon until Miss Moon eventually did a bit of a gulp thing and said, "OK."

And that's when Miss Moon told us that she WASN'T a werewolf and that werewolves didn't actually exist (as far as she knew) and that the reason she had been so GRUMPY was because she wasn't enjoying the OUTDOORS very much and that she hadn't had enough PROTEIN.

Zach asked Miss Moon about RUNNING in the woods and the SMILING as she ran and her SUPER STRENGTH. And Miss Moon said that she went for a run EVERY DAY and that she'd been smiling because exercise makes her FEEL BETTER and released POSITIVE FEELINGS and also because when we saw her she'd just run into the village and had a bacon roll.

But then Jodi said that didn't explain the HAIRINESS and Miss Jones smiled a tiny bit and Miss Moon gave her a LOOK.

Miss Moon's face went red again and she said that she might have been struggling a bit with TENT LIFE and that camping in the wild had TAKEN ITS TOLL on her. And that even though she may have looked a bit more HAIRY than normal it wasn't POLITE of us to point it out. And Miss Jones nodded in agreement but she was still smirking a little bit even though I could tell that she was trying not to.

That's when Miss Moon said that she'd been SO MISERABLE about not getting any sleep because of the

WILD BEASTS

that were TERRORISING her that she had decided it would be best for everyone if she booked herself into one of the LUXURY CARAVANS so that she could be more comfortable and get back to feeling like her usual self because camping really wasn't her cup of tea.

But then I said that didn't explain her **MEAT OBSESSION** and why she had stood in the rain for ages trying to get the barbecue to work and why she ate like **ONE HUNDRED** burgers and no buns. And her **GLOWING WEREWOLF EYES** when we did the **HAM TEST**. And the **TREE SCRATCHES**. And the **GIANT POO!**

Miss Moon said that the tree scratches might have been made by a **RABBIT** or maybe even a **WILD CAT** and she had **NO IDEA** who the **GIANT POO** belonged to but that we shouldn't go near it again and Miss Jones agreed.

Then Miss Moon said that she just really liked meat and that she was on a FULL PROTEIN DIET. And then she got a bit cross about the Ham Roof Thing and said that foxes had SURROUNDED HER TENT that night because of all the ham and that it must have been FOX EYES we saw.

I felt a bit bad when Miss Moon told us that because I knew Miss Moon must have been stuck in her tent all night listening to loads of foxes eat two hundred slices of ham off her tent and that must have been scary.

So I said sorry and so did Zach and Jodi and Maisie. And Gary Petrie said sorry, too, even though he wasn't even part of the Ham Plan.

Then Miss Jones said, "SPEAKING of MEAT. Were those the MISSING SAUSAGES we just saw the foxes run off with?!"

Miss Moon put her head down a bit and she didn't say anything and we all knew that meant that they WERE and that she had STOLEN THE SAUSAGES for herself.

That's when Miss Moon said, "I'm so sorry. I'm sorry about EVERYTHING. I've not been very good on this trip, have I?"

But nobody said anything because it seemed like one of those questions that you're not meant to answer.

Miss Moon said that she HATED camping and that the only reason she'd suggested it was because she'd heard that everyone in our class REALLY wanted to go on a school trip and she had been trying to make us happy.

And that's when I realised that even though Miss Moon is a bit of a MOAN, she was actually a nice person for taking us on a trip and obviously not a werewolf.

The next day when we were packing up Maisie started **CRYING** because she said that she **"LOVED IT HERE"** and that she didn't want to go and we all **BURST** out laughing because we hadn't expected her to say that after everything we'd been through!

When it was time to get on the bus Jodi RAN on so that she could SECURE the Bus Sofa for us and I waited with Maisie so she could take one last look around one of her "FAVOURITE PLACES IN THE WORLD"

As the bus was pulling away, Maisie opened the little Bus Curtains and looked out. And then she said, "Goodbye campsite! Goodbye barbecue bit! Goodbye wooden benches! Goodbye den-in-the-woods! Goodbye woods! Goodbye … GARY?!!"

I thought Maisie meant the RIVER GARRY but then Maisie screamed, "STOP! STOP!!" and we all looked out the back window and saw that GARY PETRIE was RUNNING AFTER THE BUS!

Miss Moon shouted, "STOP THIS BUS!"

to the bus driver and he slammed the brakes on.

Miss Moon and Miss Jones RAN down the

aisle and off the bus to get Gary and even though we couldn't hear what they were saying to Gary it looked like he was getting told off for not being on the bus.

Then Miss Moon gave Miss Jones a hug and I knew that it was because they were both REALLY HAPPY that they hadn't accidentally left without one of their pupils because they probably would have got sacked or sent to jail for that so they were obviously MEGA RELIEVED.

Everyone clapped when Gary Petrie got on the bus and he did loads of bows.

Maisie said that Gary could sit with us on

the Bus Sofa and asked him where he had been.

I thought that Gary had probably just been down at the River Garry sign, kissing it goodbye or trying to chop it down and take it home with him.

But then Gary smiled and opened his hand out in front of Jodi.

And Jodi FROZE and I know for a FACT that she thought it was going to be a BOGEY (also known as a CRUSTY SURPRISE) because Gary Petrie is usually like that.

But it wasn't.

It was JODI'S LOCKET!

Jodi looked TOTALLY SHOCKED for AGES and then she said, "OH! OH! How did you find it?! THANK YOU! WOW! THANK YOU!"

Then Gary started saying loads of random stuff about the "WHISPERING RIVER" and his "RIVER KING SENSES" and Maisie giggled loads.

EVENTUALLY Gary explained that he had gone HUNTING for it after breakfast and that he'd found it in the grass beside the River Garry sign. And that's when I remembered that Jodi had DROPPED AND CRAWLED under the sign when she found the **RED GLOVE** in the scavenger hunt.

Maisie gave Gary a hug and yelled

**"THREE CHEERS
–FOR THE RIVER GARRY!"–**

and everyone on the bus gave three cheers
and we all burst out laughing.

Acknowledgements

Love, pugs and thanks to Nola, Theo and Elliot for coming along to Kilicrankie that day to do WEREWOLF RESEARCH. Who knew we'd find a horribly wobbly ear-shaped BLOOD MUSHROOM?!

I'd also like to give a great big THANK YOU to Nicola and Thomas for the FANTASTIC design and illustrations, and to my editor, Kirsty, for being awesome as always.

Most of all, I'd like to thank my husband, Andy, for being terrified of wolves. If he didn't have nightmares about wolves (and dinosaurs!) chasing him, this book may never have happened.

Turn over for a SNEAK PEEK
of Izzy's HILARIOUS
retelling of 'Hamlet' in

TO
WEE
OR
NOT TO
WEE!

One time when we were playing Monopoly at Maisie's house we couldn't even get started because Zach COULD NOT decide if he wanted to be the hat or the car. And he kept saying stuff like, "But I like both. What should I do?" and "What if I pick the car and then I lose?" and "What if Jodi gets the car and she wins?"

Then Maisie's mum came in and asked us if we would like pepperoni on our pizza and I said yes and so did Maisie and Jodi but Zach said that he wasn't sure. And then he put his head in his hands because he couldn't decide about the car OR the hat OR

the pepperoni and it was

So that's when I told Zach that he was being **EXACTLY** like **HAMLET** out of the Shakespeare play. And Zach said that he **WASN'T** and Maisie's mum burst out laughing and said that he was, actually. Then Zach said that he

So I asked Zach if he knew who Hamlet was

and he said he didn't.

So that's when I told Zach that Hamlet was the Prince of Denmark who had been at university for about twenty years because he couldn't decide what to be when he grew up so just kept going back to college and doing LOADS of stuff like history and biology and hairdressing.

But one day when Hamlet came home to get his mum to do his washing for him he found out that his dad, the King of Denmark, had died. And then his mum told him that she was going on a date with his Uncle Claudius and that there was some left-over lasagne in the fridge.

Hamlet was FURIOUS because his mum didn't even seem BOTHERED that his dad had died and also because she was going on a date with HIS UNCLE (which was TOTALLY WEIRD even though she was pretending that it wasn't).

Hamlet's mum and his Uncle Claudius got back from their date JUST in time for the king's funeral and as SOON as the funeral finished Claudius went down on one knee and PROPOSED to Hamlet's mum! Then he told all the funeral guests to just stay sitting down because they were about to

get MARRIED and he was going to be the
KING OF DENMARK!

Hamlet was totally SHOCKED because his
uncle was about to become his STEPDAD

and also because HE was supposed to become King of Denmark. And he probably should have grabbed the minister's microphone and shouted, "Mum! You CAN'T marry Dad's BROTHER! That's disgusting!" and also "I'M THE KING NOW!"

But Hamlet didn't shout any of those things. He just sat there trying to decide what to do to stop the wedding until the minister said, "I now pronounce you husband and wife," and it was too late.